To Ja
li
Best:
Sarah E Zilkowski

BEASTS
of WAR

A RETELLING OF
THE OLD ENGLISH JUDITH

SARAH E ZILKOWSKI

Publishing services provided by  **Archangel Ink**
Making Publishing A Reality

ISBN: 978-1-950043-39-2

To all of my past teachers, especially

Thomas Laird, my first Creative Writing teacher,

Dr. Stella Singer, my graduate advisor,

and

Dr. Susan Kim, who introduced me

to the world and stories of the Anglo-Saxons

DISCLAIMER

The cover artwork was taken from an oil on canvas painting created by Cristofano Allori in 1613 entitled *Judith With the Head of Holofernes*. It is in the public domain and was adapted for *Beasts of War* by Archangel Ink Publishing. While the cover image depicts Judith as she is described in the apocryphal Old Testament story, it should be noted that Allori's painting was an adapted work too. It is said that the heads of the characters resemble those of Maria de Giovanni Mazzafirri - a woman he loved (Judith), her mother (the maid), and himself (Holofernes). The painting is part of a canon of well-thought out and detailed adaptations of the Judith story. Since *Beasts of War* retells *Judith* from a new and different perspective, it seemed only fitting to highlight another creator who has done the same.

If you are interested in learning more about Anglo-Saxon literature, history and culture, or upcoming publications by Sarah E Zilkowski, sign-up at **JudithBook.com** for updates.

CONTENTS

AUTHOR'S NOTE

Modern societies have long had a fascination with ancient civilizations. There are many cultures that died out millennia ago, and yet we still know them intimately through the writing, artifacts, and buildings, ruined or otherwise, left behind by the people of these societies. The Greeks, Egyptians, Ancient Chinese, and Mesopotamians were all societies that flourished for centuries and today are not only remembered with remarkable detail but are even revered. Many historians argue that we must preserve the memory of these cultures in today's world to understand who we are and where we come from, but for every ancient culture that is remembered, numerous others vanished without notice.

Today, English is one of the most commonly recognized languages, thanks in part to the United States of America, whose native English language has a global reach in foreign affairs and economic trade. However, before the USA spread her influence, England was the world superpower colonizing foreign lands and establishing trade routes during its age of exploration. The effects of England's colonization can still be seen on nearly every continent across the globe: North America (United States and Canada); Europe; Asia (India); Africa (South Africa); Australia; even the northern part of South America was under British influence, while several Caribbean islands are still occupied by Britain. England spread its culture far and wide.

Ironically, though this small country has made a great impact on the world, we barely know more than 1,500 years of its history. The original Britons are a mystery, and the Celtic people before them are even more aloof. There are few, if any, records of the inhabitants of Britain before the Romans settled sometime between 41 and 49 AD, extending their empire as far west as it would ever go.

The Romans remained on the island for about 300 years when the collapse of the empire forced them to retreat to mainland Europe. During the years of occupation, Britannia was a Roman territory in every sense of the word. Latin was spoken as often as any common tongue. Roman architecture and infrastructure were employed extensively. Roads were well cared for and ran in intricate configurations connecting one part of the island to the other. The economy used Roman currency, and even the sewer systems and water aqueducts resembled those of prosperous Rome.

Certain structures from that era still remain, including portions of Hadrian's Wall, which was built to keep out the wild and warring northern tribes of Scotland—particularly the Picts—from attacking the more civilized cities and towns of the south under Roman rule. A Roman bathhouse can still be found in Bath, England. Today it stands as a museum with multiple rooms, nearly as complete as it was when it was in use.

When the Romans left the island, they took their armies with them because they were needed closer to the capital. Those who remained were largely defenseless against the northern tribes. In the decades that followed, the Britons found it hard to defend their lands against those tribes and their particular brand of warfare. To help compensate for lack of soldiers, Vortigern, one of the well-known lords at the time, invited the Angles, Saxons, and

Jutes from modern-day Norway, Denmark, and Iceland to come and assist in defending against the northern peoples in 449 AD. The foreigners agreed to immigrate to Britain and traveled by boat *en masse* to help defend the country.

And so, the era of the Anglo-Saxons began in England. It was a time when the spoken word was held in higher regard than the written one, a broken promise could cost a man his life, and fighting was the quickest way to acquire wealth.

When the Angles, Saxons, and Jutes arrived, they quickly made the island home. They developed a new culture that blended characteristics from their Germanic/Scandinavian homeland as well as Christianity, which allowed them to create a society with traditions, ideals, and characteristics that were distinctly their own. They also developed their own language, a cross between the high Germanic languages of Europe and the Latin and Celtic languages that still remained in Britain.

Their culture was rich and vibrant, thanks to their skilled craftsmen and artisans. Their government was clan-based. Each village/society was ruled by a lord whose *thanes*, warriors, had the responsibility to not only defend their own territory but defeat other lords and their armies; take their gold, jewels, and precious metals; and assimilate the conquered people into their own society. Every time a lord and his thanes defeated others, it made them more powerful and the whole village wealthier.

No man ran from a fight. They lived by the code of the *comitatus*, a term coined by the Roman Tacitus in *Germania*, written in approximately 98 AD after he visited the Germanic tribes outside the Roman Empire in mainland Europe. The cultural similarities of the *comitatus* bond of the Germanic peoples and the Anglo-Saxons could be assumed through later writings. Each thane fought for his lord, never backing down from a fight. If a lord died in the midst of battle, his thanes were expected to continue fighting and avenge his death.

If a thane did retreat, he was banished from the community as an outcast, destined to wander for the rest of his life. It was rare for another community to take him in. No one wanted a traitor in their community. Instead, the woods became his home. Danger was everywhere, and no one was expected to survive the elements and animals easily on his own. In a culture where community and loyalty were so highly revered, banishment to the woods was often thought of as a fate worse than death.

Perhaps the safest and happiest place for the Anglo-Saxons was the mead hall. This was where the community would gather for celebrations, and these celebrations always included food, stories, and mead. The stories were told by *scops*, men who learned to play instruments and tell tales through song. Some stories, like *Beowulf*, spoke of their homeland while others recounted recent battles won. Battle tales were often embellished to make the victory appear especially glorious.

It was not until Christianity was established on the island at the end of the sixth century that monasteries were developed, and where there are monasteries… there are written records and books. Soon, more and more events were recorded in print. In addition to Christian writings copied from Latin texts, the monks also wrote in the vernacular. In the centuries before the fall of the Anglo-Saxon era, extensive libraries were established under the rule of Alfred the Great. Monks were employed solely for the creation and transcription of books, and even some lay people were literate. This period of time from 871 to 899 AD is considered by scholars to be the golden age of the Anglo-Saxons.

The texts from this era captured the stories, essays, rhymes, and poems that were popular among the Anglo-Saxons. Some were quite bawdy, including Riddle 44, found in the *Exeter Book*: "It hangs, elegant, high on his thigh/ Under his shirt, with a hole in the front./ It stands upright, stiff and hard!/ When he takes it out of his clothes, intending/ To use it, he'll stick the head of his hanging/ Thing straight in that matching hole/ That he's filled in this way so often before." (Trans. Raffel & Olson, 1998).

Though the riddle initially seems to describe the male anatomy, the answer to the seven-line poem is actually a *key*. The clues were so cleverly crafted that the riddle has stood the test of time and even been shared in modern publications.

There were also stories, such as the epic poem of *Judith*, which were adapted from Christian tradition to include Anglo-Saxon characteristics. Many of the details are different, but the overarching plot and main ideas of the Anglo-Saxon text are largely modeled after the original source.

The Judith of the apocryphal Old Testament book is a widow. However, in the Anglo-Saxon story she is a beautiful, young virgin—a maiden held in high esteem by society. In the Old Testament story, little is known of her appearance, but the Anglo-Saxon poem gives her characteristics that were popular during that period, most notably her golden hair fashioned into a long braid. Anglo-Saxon words such as *idesse,* meaning a woman who is more than a queen but less than a goddess ("fairy-like") are used to describe her. On the other hand, the villain, Holofernes, is seen as a monster—a heathen dog, a motif used for Anglo-Saxon villains time and again.

The wolf, raven, and eagle appear before and after the battle scenes of the Judith poem. These are the Anglo-Saxon beasts of war. No fight scene is complete without at least one of these animals making an appearance, and if they show up in a story, readers know a battle is imminent.

Though a fair amount is known today about the culture, the Anglo-Saxons were forgotten for centuries. After William the Conqueror, a Norman man by birth, defeated Harold Godwinson at the Battle of Hastings on October 14, 1066, and became the new ruler of England, the new aristocracy was not interested in learning English. The upper and lower classes were quickly divided by language as well as other socio-economic variables, and the Old English language and its stories were no longer recorded. Those who established themselves as the aristocracy preferred to read and hear stories about the first Britons and Celts, and this is how the Arthurian legends were born. King Arthur was known as the king of the Britons during a mythical time before the Anglo-Saxons arrived. While the legends of Arthur and the stories of newer writers advanced in popularity, the manuscripts of the Anglo-Saxons were abandoned and largely forgotten.

While several minor Anglo-Saxon manuscripts have been preserved over the years, the four major poetic Anglo-Saxons manuscripts still in existence are the *Junius Manuscript*, *Exeter Book*, *Vercelli Book*, and *Nowell Codex*. From these four texts we get the bulk of our literary knowledge of the Anglo-Saxons.

The *Nowell Codex* included both the epic poems *Beowulf* and *Judith*. However, the manuscript suffered heavy damage in 1731 when the Cotton Library, where it was being stored, caught fire. Though the book was saved, large portions of both stories are missing. The story of *Judith* is believed to have been damaged at the beginning and end. While some scholars argue that huge portions of the manuscript are missing, others believe that only a few lines of verse have been lost.

Old English stories were always written in verse and often left out the dialogue and details that can be found in our modern novels. Because of these characteristics, I was inspired to take on the task of turning these Old English poems into stories, particularly novels, which today's readers can appreciate. I spent nearly half of my undergraduate and my entire graduate careers studying Old English—*Judith* in particular. Under the direction of my professors, I personally translated the 300+ line poem and wrote a master's thesis on the text.

I hold the Anglo-Saxon Judith, just like the Anglo-Saxon culture, in high esteem, and I feel it is time her story was shared with the world. One thing to remember, though, is that her story was adapted from the Old Testament. Because of this, Judith and Holofernes are the only two characters in the poem who were given names. These names, along with Bethulia—the name of the city Judith resided in—retained their Jewish/Assyrian origins.

The Anglo-Saxons did not have a problem incorporating details, names, and ideas from other cultures into their stories. An Anglo-Saxon listening to the story of *Judith* would have felt at ease with the anachronisms we sometimes find so jarring in our culture. These details were of little consequence, and the majority of the story or poem took on the cultural characteristics of the period.

In this novel, I have given all the characters Anglo-Saxon names, but I have retained the names of Judith, Holofernes, and Bethulia to keep in line with the original Anglo-Saxon text. Additionally, many liberties have been taken with the story. Whereas villains in Anglo-Saxon literature have no redeeming qualities, and heroes have few (if any) flaws, Holofernes has positive (even human) attributes, and Judith does have flaws. Besides, certain additions have been made to all chapters. Some chapters, such as the journey to Holofernes's camp and the days Judith spent there, were scenes not even described in the original poem, but these details were necessary to turn the poem into a cohesive novel.

Though I took some liberties, my intent is to retain as much of the Anglo-Saxon culture as possible in an effort to introduce this rich and vibrant era to modern readers. Theirs was a beautiful and fierce culture, one I feel deeply connected to. This is why I have attempted to give the Anglo-Saxon world and its literature a voice in the modern world by adapting and sharing their stories with you.

To you, the reader:

While the historical information in this author's note is accurate, it does not encompass the entirety of the rich history of the Anglo-Saxons. Most notably, the influence of the Vikings has been left out; only those areas that are pertinent to the story of Judith are highlighted. Many scholars have devoted their entire careers to studying and writing about the history and literature of the Anglo-Saxon era, and I encourage every reader to seek out these authors and illuminate yourself on the vibrant Anglo-Saxon world modern scholarship has uncovered.

While this story was written to showcase Anglo-Saxon culture through a prose adaptation of an Anglo-Saxon epic poem, it was also written to entertain. Although not wholly accurate in every capacity, I hope that this colorful Anglo-Saxon story might spark in you a love for a culture that is so little understood, yet so deserving of being remembered.

—Sarah E Zilkowski

PROLOGUE

The smoke grew thick around the town. The farms and fields that had gone up in flames hours before were now smoldering. Many of the thanes had been killed. Only a few remained, boldly facing their enemies as they continued to clash swords and swing battle axes. They were exhausted after two days of fighting.

Their lord had fallen at the end of the first day. A swinging sword had slashed his neck wide open. Grasping at his wound, he lost his balance and fell off his horse. The great man who had won countless battles and lived a life of valor was trampled by an enemy stallion.

The lord died bravely, as all lords should, unafraid of the men threatening his home. He had fought valiantly, but he was an old man past his prime. Nevertheless, he stared death in the face, knowing he had done his duty for his people.

His thanes saw his defeat and rallied. They continued to fight to avenge their lord until they, too, perished. By the end of the second day, the remaining thanes were outnumbered five to one, and the odds of victory were slim. The soldiers fought on honorably as the dead piled around them.

When the last of the defending army was cut down, the enemy

turned its attention to the town where the farmers and tradesmen were protecting the women and children. The townspeople had heard rumors of a terrifying lord traveling across the country, destroying everything in his path. The stories said his army was large enough to destroy whole villages, killing both women and children. Now they saw firsthand that the rumors were true, but they did not live long enough to warn others.

The enemy destroyed all cities and towns that offered resistance, and they killed everyone, beginning with the men. As the children and women ran to hide, the soldiers made a sport of hunting them down. Houses were turned upside down as the men searched the far corners for those in hiding. Despite their fatigue from the battle, a dozen thanes rode into the forest to track down those who tried to run. They showed no mercy. To them, everyone was an enemy, even those who could not defend themselves. Children were killed as brutally as their parents. Women were raped and left with their throats slashed open.

Soon, death covered the village. It was then that Holofernes, the great leader of the savage army, came forward, surveyed the wreckage, and gave out his orders.

"Collect the town's gold, silver, jewelry, and all valuable items. Butcher what animals you can, save the horses, and burn the pens. Pillage the huts and burn the town to the ground when we leave. You," he barked to Knut, one of his bravest thanes, "torch the mead hall. We'll use its light to work. Go. Now."

At his command, the men scattered, and the mead hall was set alight. It had been a dry season and the timber shot up in flames at once.

Acwel was one of the thanes assigned the task of going from house to house looking for valuables. As he reached a home in a far corner of the town, he paused. From inside he could hear the faintest tune… someone was singing, and the voice was beautiful. He set aside his torch and entered the home, which appeared empty.

"Who's there?" he called, but he was met with silence. He began a search of the house. It did not take long to find two children under the bed—a girl, no older than five, who was clutching a rag doll, and an older boy, who looked nearly identical to her. Acwel guessed him to be about ten. *Around the same age as my boy*, he noted. The children stared at him with tears in their eyes.

"Were you singing to her just now?" he asked. The children had matted, bloody hair, terrified eyes, and ghostly pale skin. Only hours before, they'd witnessed a man plunge a dagger deep into their mother's heart, and they were afraid of the fate that awaited them.

"Answer me," he screamed in their faces.

The boy gave a nearly imperceptible nod.

Without another word, Acwel grabbed them by their red hair and dragged them out into the open. On their way out, he picked up the torch and lit the roof on fire. Then he brought the children to the center of town for all the men to see.

The children began to kick and scream, but the thanes tied their hands and feet together and presented them to their lord. The girl dropped her doll and wet herself at the sight of the man. Not only was he a giant by comparison to most, but his sly smile and the gleam in his eyes were terrifying to behold. The boy was brave, and though his body shook with fear, he met the lord's gaze without backing down. With a laugh, the warlord picked the girl up and threw her into the mead hall fire.

"Mayda!" the boy screamed, but Acwel held the boy tightly so he was unable to move.

The great lord looked down at the boy. "What a lovely name

she had. What's yours?"

The child barely heard him as he stood in horror watching his sister burn. Holofernes grabbed his shoulders and shook him hard. "What's your name?" he roared, inches from the boy's face.

"Rowe," the boy just managed to whisper.

"Ah…" the lord muttered and turned back to the fire. He laughed as the flames engulfed the small maiden and stifled her cries. The army stood by, laughing at her torture too. It did not take long for the girl to inhale the smoke, and she was dead. Her body was left roasting in the mead hall, the place that was supposed to offer comfort and security above all others.

Holofernes made a move to grab Rowe next, but the ache in Acwel's heart at missing his own son overcame him. "My lord," he said, causing the army leader to pause. "This one can sing. I overheard him. His voice is beautiful. Perhaps he can be of use to us."

The lord looked down at the terrified child. "Is this true? Sing for me now."

Rowe looked from Holofernes to Acwel and back again.

"If you want to live, boy, sing," Acwel demanded.

Rowe was just about to answer when a whiff of his sister's burnt flesh reached his nose, and before he could stop himself, he retched down the front of his clothes. Anger flashed in the lord's eyes.

Still shaking, Rowe wiped his mouth and began the song Acwel had heard earlier. It was only a simple lullaby, but it was clear his voice was angelic.

"Hmm…" Holofernes said as he studied him. "Do you know any war songs? Epic tales? Bawdy drinking songs to entertain my men?"

Rowe looked down at his hands sheepishly.

"Come now, your mother isn't here. You won't get in trouble. In fact, it might save you," Acwel encouraged.

Finally, Rowe found his voice. "Yes. My father was a thane, and I would often sneak into the mead hall on nights when he ate with his lord. I learned such songs as I watched and listened in the shadows."

The sly smile once again returned to Holofernes's face. "If you are lying, I will soon find out. If you are telling the truth, you may sing for us, and we will feed, clothe, and shelter you. Release his ropes."

As Rowe's ropes were cut, he fell to the ground to grab his sister's doll. The lord took it from him and threw it to Acwel, who caught it one-handed and looked at it with sadness. In all the excitement one of the doll's eyes had come loose and fallen to the ground. As Acwel stooped to pick it up, he noticed both eyes were made from small, lopsided garnets in a color so deep red they appeared nearly black. *What an odd thing*, he thought.

"Get rid of the doll and kill him if he tries to run," Holofernes commanded. Then the lord surveyed the damage that had been done and gave a nod of approval. "In the morning we march."

CHAPTER 1

3 YEARS LATER

For years, Holofernes's army was unstoppable. News of his victories spread wildly. As the army was meticulous and methodical, those towns still untouched by Holofernes knew it wasn't a question of whether his army would appear at their gates, but when.

Some days before Holofernes's army appeared at Bethulia's famous walls, the guards of the city saw billowing black smoke rise from their nearest neighbor. It was the only town standing between them and the dreaded enemy. What concerned them even more, though, was that their dear lord was lying feebly on his deathbed. Godwine, the old lord, had been sick for days with a fever that kept growing hotter. He was an aged man undefeated in battle. His people had hoped his last fight would be with Holofernes's army, but it was obvious that was not to be. Delusions began to overtake his mind. He spoke of things that didn't make sense, and reality slipped further away with each passing day.

As the flames of the nearby village grew high into the sky, the lord, with his only son by his side, came back to his senses one last time. When he saw Cyneric in front of him, Godwine placed his son's strong hand in his own shaky one. Then he kissed his boy and with a raspy whisper said, "You will rule when I am gone. Rule as your ancestors did, with courage and compassion."

There was a long pause as Godwine stared into Cyneric's face, trying to memorize it one last time. Finally, he continued, even weaker than before. "I am now off to see your mother." Then the old lord, without much ado, closed his eyes and breathed his last.

All at once, devastation and fear washed over Cyneric. He was the new lord of the town, but he was young. He felt unprepared. At that same moment, a guard who had just been relieved from the watchtower came over and knelt beside him. He gave a low bow to Lord Godwine, his leader even in death, and then looked to his new lord.

"The great army has just destroyed our neighbor. We have seen their fires and can smell the smoke of the defeated town even from here. It will not be long before the enemy marches on us."

Without stopping to think of the consequences, Cyneric gave his first command. "Close the gate. Lock it securely. No one is to come in or go out. Once the army has seen the city walls are impenetrable, it will move on to the next town."

The guard looked confused. To retreat was not the way of their people, and he did not understand what the boy was thinking. However, he could see Cyneric's grief and did not question him. Instead, he went out and ordered the guards to lock the gate securely.

"No one is to enter or leave until Lord Cyneric gives the command."

The morning after Lord Godwine died, the townspeople saw that Holofernes's army was setting up camp in the open field along the forest's edge just half a day's march away. Cyneric hoped the army would pass by after a few days. However, after several weeks, it was clear they had no intention of leaving, and the Bethulians were running out of provisions. As lord, Cyneric did what he could to ration the food and keep his people calm and content, but he knew their current situation could not last forever.

Cyneric felt uncertain of his people's future, and even more uncertain of his own. In truth, he'd never wanted to be lord, not really. The responsibility had always seemed too grave. To gain the position now, at a time when all felt hopeless and defeat seemed imminent, was the very last thing he wanted. He felt lost and alone, and there were few he could turn to for guidance.

It was clear his inaction was causing him to lose favor with his people, who were all still grieving Godwine's death. Cyneric had always felt inadequate in his father's great shadow. The man was a legend. He had been so successful at claiming peace for his people that Cyneric had never once been sent into battle. No one had dared fight Godwine and his thanes in decades. Their valor and skill was too superior, and peaceful negotiations with a ruler as wise as Godwine were always welcome. Cyneric doubted he could ever be as successful as the man who had come before him, and it was clear from the whisperings of the thanes and advisors who were now in his service that they believed the same.

***

One of Godwine's closest friends, a man he loved like a brother, had been Deorwine. He was a merchant who regularly traveled to the coast to meet the traders, and he always returned with the most exquisite goods and tantalizing stories. Deorwine was well loved by the Bethulian people and was known far and wide. Deorwine's wife died young, leaving him with one child, a girl by the name of Judith. The small family had a nursemaid, Nerienda, who lived with them and ensured Judith was looked after when Deorwine traveled to the coast.

Deorwine often ventured across the sea to the eastern lands and bartered there for unique and beautiful materials not found near Bethulia. The ornate objects he encountered were almost as interesting as the merchants selling them. At night, after the market closed for the day, Deorwine would sit with those same merchants, many of whom were twice his age, and listen as they told fantastic tales of their most memorable journeys.

When Deorwine returned from his travels, everyone from Bethulia and the nearby towns would come to see him at the stand where he sold his wares. However, the stories he had heard while on his travels were even more anticipated than the ornaments he put on display. Whenever he started telling a story, everyone within earshot would stop what they were doing and gather around to listen.

His most captivated audience member, though, was always Judith. When Deorwine began his stories, she would stop whatever game she was playing and climb up on her father's lap to listen. Despite her young age, she could sit and listen to him all day, entranced by the tales of strange men, frightening monsters, and heroic feats of strength. Her father's stories painted pictures of far-off lands that were so vivid she may as well have been there herself.

Judith had few companions growing up; Cyneric, the lord's son, was her only close playmate. The two children were good friends, just like their fathers. They played together in the town and surrounding fields and became one another's confidants as they grew older. Both grew up without a mother and both were known to be a bit awkward compared to the rest of the children. Together, though, they made a handsome pair, and as close friends do, they watched out for each other. Everyone assumed their love would grow naturally and that Judith would be Cyneric's bride one day.

When Judith was eleven, Deorwine set out on a journey to Normandy and never came back. Months later, a traveling merchant stopped by the town giving news that sometime back a ship traveling to the Norman coast had capsized in a storm and all were lost.

With a heavy heart, Nerienda began to raise Judith on her own, and the two lived quietly in a far corner of the town. In her grief, Judith cut herself off from others, even from her closest friend, and spent her days at home in solitude. After her father's death, the town no longer felt like home. Her grief was so profound that others didn't have the heart to interrupt her and left her alone in isolation. As the years went on, she felt more and more like an outsider forced to live within the boundaries of a foreign land.

It was during this time that Judith's grief was eventually comforted by her faith. Her people had converted to the religion of the missionaries from the east long ago when her father's father was a small child, and though it was steeped in the traditions of their pagan homeland—loyalty, honor, and duty toward one's people—the Christian God and His dogma reigned. Through her fervent prayer, her faith grew stronger with each passing year. Most people had no idea of the long hours she spent beseeching heaven, but Cyneric knew. He would occasionally see her out in the fields and on the forest's edge, in the places that had been favorites of theirs. He would watch protectively from a distance as she offered prayers and petitions for the people of her town. She no longer felt like a part of her own community, but duty required that she pray for them as much as herself. Faith and loyalty went hand in hand, and she was nothing if not faithful. Cyneric never got close to her, never once asked her why she shut herself away from the world and from him. He understood. The pain she felt was immense, but he hoped one day she would come around to see her old friend again.

She never did, though. For seven years, Judith lived this way. The night Lord Godwine died, she had been taking a walk through the town, praying for her lord and waiting for his soul to pass. She had known he was ill, and once he died, the news traveled quickly. When the whispers reached her, she said one final prayer before turning back to her hut. As she stepped through the streets, she could smell the fire burning several miles away.

"Judith," Nerienda rushed to her side as she entered their home. "I was so worried. Where were you?"

"Over by our lord's home," she said.

"Has he passed?"

"Yes," Judith whispered.

The maid made the sign of the cross over her body. "May his soul find rest in the Lord's great mead hall. But right now there is more to be concerned with. Holofernes and his army have just taken the town to the north of us, and Cyneric ordered the gates locked. No one is to leave or enter Bethulia. I was terrified you were out by the forest and unable to get back in."

Judith gave her maid a reassuring look and held the old woman's hands in hers. "Don't be worried," she said. "I am here, and we are safe."

Then she quietly left the hut and climbed up onto its roof. She did this often at night when she wanted to look at the stars. When other people saw her, they always thought it was peculiar behavior, but Judith enjoyed it. It put her just high enough so that all she could see in front of her were the towering walls of the town, the stars in the night sky, and the moon shining down. She felt closer to her father when she was there, closer to her mother whom she'd never known. She could pray more easily, and the troubles of the world disappeared for a short time. This was where Judith felt most at peace, and it didn't matter what other people thought.

Judith stayed on the roof for most of the night praying for Godwine's soul. She prayed the lord was once again united with all his family and friends who passed before him, especially her father. She also prayed that Cyneric might be comforted. Grief, she knew, was a heavy burden, and she hoped the weight of it would not hinder his ability to lead their people.

Most nights the roof was peaceful, but tonight thick black smoke filled the sky, nearly blocking out the moon and half the stars. The smell of the smoldering nearby town filled the air, and the unmistakable stench of burnt flesh made the gloom of Bethulia even heavier. With tears in her eyes, Judith prayed for all the families destroyed by Holofernes's latest victory.

After several long, tearful hours, Judith crept back down into the house, where Nerienda was fast asleep. She lay down in her own bed, but sleep did not come easily. She felt as though some big change was about to occur—something more than the impending battle everyone was worrying about. When at last she was finally able to dream, her sleep was filled with nightmares. However, by morning, she had forgotten about the unusual premonition and the dreams of the night before as she and the rest of Bethulia set out to secure their town against a terrifying enemy.

In the days that followed, Judith found herself on the roof more frequently, praying for the people of Bethulia. As the weeks wore on and still nothing changed, her prayers became more focused and fervent. Over and over again she repeated, "Lord or lords, you sent your Son to deliver us from evil. Send a savior now to deliver us from the demons outside our walls and the despair that covers us within them."

CHAPTER 2

As the weeks passed, the townspeople's worry turned into frustration and then anger. There was talk of overthrowing the lord and setting one of the thanes in his place. However, out of respect for Godwine, they refrained. Even in death, a great leader rules through the memories of his people, and that is exactly what was happening in Bethulia.

Everyone agreed that Cyneric was young and immature, but they hoped he would soon unveil a plan for them to fight against Holofernes. People were starving as they awaited Cyneric's guidance. Wheat had to be rationed and meat was almost never available. The produce of the land came to them only in meager quantities through a secret entrance. Even water and mead were running low. Sadly, though, no new orders were given, and discontentment spread through the streets as quickly as the mead dried up.

One of the most troubling sights for Judith was watching her young neighbor, Ellette—a girl no more than four—turn from a rambunctious, happy, playful child into a lethargic wisp of a being with hollow eyes and a somber countenance. Judith and Ellette had formed a kind of friendship in recent years.

The child was fearless and unbothered by decorum. While the

rest of the townspeople kept their distance from Judith and her quiet life, Ellette often interrupted her neighbor to say hello or share a story. More than once when Judith had been alone on her roof, Ellette had yelled up to her and interrupted her prayers. The girl would often leave wildflowers on Judith's doorstep. In return, Judith would gift her feathers or pretty rocks, the two things Ellette was always collecting, when she saw her playing outside. The girl was sweet but wild, and Judith loved her free-spirited ways. It pained her that the siege had transformed Ellette so dramatically. Food was so scarce that even the children were lucky to get one small meal a day. Judith often shared her own meager meals with her little friend, and the sweet girl took the food with heartfelt appreciation. However, the few extra morsels did little to satiate the appetite of a growing girl.

***

Spring gave way to summer, and summer's long days quickly drew to a close with little change. The leaves were just beginning to turn from emerald green to crimson red when the farmers brought word to Cyneric that there was almost nothing left. The season should have produced a rich harvest, but since Holofernes had set up camp as the spring rains began, very little had been planted and most of it was destroyed or consumed by the enemy army. Instead of the abundance the Bethulians were used to, the harvest brought very little yield to the tables of the townspeople.

Cyneric listened quietly while the grave matter was presented. With a somber heart, he dismissed the farmers and told them to keep the news quiet. Then he locked himself in his room. He'd spent the past months searching for answers, desperate to find a way to beat Holofernes, but nothing he or his advisors came up with held any promise. If they opened their gates now, it would mean defeat. If they stayed locked away, death. Cyneric's body heaved with heavy sobs, and he fell to the floor. After months of resistance, he finally gave in to his fears. Eventually, his head cleared, and his mind became quiet. He sat in silence, waiting for an answer.

Go to Judith, a voice whispered from deep in his heart.

No, his head immediately shouted back. He had not spoken to his friend in years, and the thought of going to her made him deeply anxious.

Send her. The voice in his heart persisted. *She can kill him. His sheep will be lost without him, and your army will be victorious.*

Cyneric had his doubts. He admitted that sending in a spy could work, but he trusted no one. *Except Judith*, the voice interrupted his thoughts.

"Except Judith," he acquiesced. The thought of meeting up with his old friend caused his hands to shake. He still cared deeply for her, but he had no way of knowing how she felt toward him. He was unsure how she would respond to him. Despite his fears, though, he trusted her. He always would.

***

Shortly after, on a dark night when the moon was new and the air was crisp with the changing of the seasons, Judith was interrupted in her nightly rooftop prayers by a knock below. There were a few whispered words of greeting before Nerienda ushered Cyneric into their home and offered him a seat at the table. Though she offered what food they had, Cyneric did not take more than a few sips of mead before asking if he could speak with Judith.

"Of course, my lord," Nerienda replied, embarrassed that Judith was not in the house. "Let me just step outside to get her."

Nerienda found Judith already on solid ground, brushing the dust off her cloak. The old woman gave her a telling look. As always, she pretended not to see Nerienda's gaze and smiled sweetly as she walked into the house.

Judith had no idea what Cyneric wanted, but she knew that for him to come to her, especially at such a late hour, was not typical behavior of a lord. She sat down across from him at the table and waited patiently for him to speak, but Cyneric kept silent for a long while. Judith began to wonder if he was going to say anything at all. He looked as if he might just get up and leave without speaking a word. Finally, though, he cleared his throat and began.

"Judith, you know as well as any that our city is falling into ruin. The great walls my grandfather built have kept Holofernes's army out and our people safe these past months, but we are slowly being destroyed from within. People are starving. Children are ill. Strong men are becoming weak, and women have turned so frail that several have suffered miscarriages. We will all die unless we open the gates and receive assistance from our neighbors to the south. However, if we do so, the army will break through our guards, and in our weakened state, I know they will destroy us."

There was a moment of silence before he continued.

"We need someone who can do something to help."

Judith began to grow uneasy, unsure where the conversation was going.

"We need someone," he continued nervously, "who can go into the enemy camp and destroy the most valuable thing they have. Once that is done, the enemy will be weak enough for our army to destroy them."

Judith thought for a moment. "What do you propose this person do?" she asked timidly.

Cyneric looked at her, more willing to speak now.

"That person must travel to the enemy camp and convince Holofernes that he is no threat. Then while he is there, he must kill him and return with some token of proof that Holofernes has been destroyed. Once this happens, our army will be renewed, and we can fight the leaderless band of men. Without their lord, the enemy will not be able to defeat us.

"Holofernes is said to be one of the best army commanders in the whole country, but it is also said that his men fear him. Men only fight for their deceased lord if he was truly loving and compassionate. No army fights for a slain lord who was brutal to them while he lived. Once Holofernes is dead, his men won't avenge him. They will retreat. At least, that is my suspicion."

Judith listened intently, unsure why Cyneric was explaining all this to her at such a late hour.

"But what man could carry out such a dangerous task?" she asked.

At the question, the young lord stared boldly into her blue eyes. He noticed a look of fervor in them.

"Judith, we have known each other for a long time. Growing up, we were best friends, and even after your father…"

Judith looked away as he spoke, fighting back the sting of tears at the mention of the past. It was hard enough to see her old friend sitting in front of her, but for Cyneric to bring up her father was more than she was prepared to handle. However, the young lord was adamant in delivering his message.

"Even after your father passed, I never stopped caring for you. Over the years, my love for you hasn't wavered, even if it has only been offered from a distance. I'm here now because you are the only person I completely trust. If I were to ask one of my father's men to carry out this deed, it would surely reach the ears of others. Something so unconventional could cause everyone to lose what little faith they have in me. Besides, the enemy will be expecting a man. We need a woman to complete this task. You must go to the army camp. You must be the one to kill Holofernes."

Judith looked at him in disbelief. *Surely, he is joking*, she thought. Before the words escaped her lips, she caught herself. Cyneric was still lord, after all. Instead, she paused and chose her words carefully.

"How can you send me? I've never even held a sword. What good would I be at a camp filled with trained men?"

"You are precisely the person to go. You are young and beautiful. It is true you may have never held a sword, but did I not share my lessons on fighting with you when we were younger? You know how to wield a dagger, and swordplay with sticks taught you the basics of combat. You know more than most women, even if those lessons ended long ago. If anyone can trick them into thinking she's not a threat, it's you. Tell them anything you want. Do whatever you have to. Just destroy Holofernes."

Judith stared at Cyneric with amazement. The audacity he had in asking her was beyond belief.

"You have faith far beyond anyone I have ever met, and with a faith so strong, I know nothing will be able to stop you," Cyneric added. "I wouldn't ask if I could see any other way, but all the other options I have run through my mind will certainly end in death for many."

"And if I fail," she whispered, "this will only end in death for me."

Cyneric was silent for a moment.

"No, that is not true. If you fail, we will all perish just like every other town Holofernes has come across. You are our best chance."

"I can't do it. I forgot how to fight long ago, and I don't have the courage," Judith argued.

"You do, Judith. When your father died and left you alone at the age of eleven, you stayed strong. You took care of yourself, and you and Nerienda were able to live together on your own. It takes a great deal of courage for a young maiden to do that. You have always shown such courage. Which of us climbed to the highest branches of the trees or swam fastest through a running current? Which of us could stand on the forest edge longest even when we could hear wolves prowling? You did, every time. You've always had courage, Judith. You might not remember, but I do. And remembering how to fight is a simple matter. Such things never really leave us. We only have to remember them in moments of danger."

Judith drew in a great breath and let it out slowly. "There's a difference between childhood games and courage and skill amidst true danger. One I have outgrown, and the other I have never possessed."

Cyneric looked at her with deep concern and pleaded in a near whisper. "Please accept this task. If you do not agree to this, I fear all will be lost."

Judith could see her old friend was desperate. She understood his strategy to send one person into the enemy camp. In truth, it was a good one. Still, she did not like her role in it. She sat pondering the options, but even as she did, she knew there was no one else in the town Cyneric could ask. *I must be a fool for even considering agreeing to this*, she thought.

"How long do I have to decide?"

The lord snapped his head up, unsure if he heard correctly, but it was clear from Judith's furrowed brow that she was serious. He let out a deep sigh.

"Take as long as you need. Just remember, the longer we wait, the more likely the army is to attack and the weaker we become."

Judith nodded. "At least let me have the night."

"Agreed," Cyneric said, too relieved to place any stipulations on her.

As the proposition of her lord spun in her ears and thoughts of battle painted dizzying images in her mind, Judith steadied herself and tried to quiet her soul. She wanted desperately to get Cyneric to leave so she could think. This was not a decision to be made lightly.

"I'll send Nerienda to you in the morning with my answer," she said.

"Very good. I will be waiting. Thank you, Judith."

"I haven't said yes yet," she replied.

"No, but you're considering it. So, thank you."

Suddenly, Cyneric took her hand in his, held it up to his lips, and kissed it softly. This was something he had done time and time again when they were young, but this kiss seemed to hold a much deeper meaning than the playful affections from years before. It was small and light, and it brought back a flood of memories and emotions she had nearly forgotten. The rush of her heart made her uncomfortable but no less affectionate toward the man before her. She had never stopped caring for him either.

Holding her hand just a moment longer, Cyneric gazed into Judith's eyes. They were still as beautiful as he remembered, but today they held a sorrow he hadn't seen before. *Then again,* he thought, *I suppose mine do too.* He released her hand and prepared to depart for home, but as he made his way to the door, he suddenly stopped and turned back with sincere earnestness.

"I know with God's grace, you will succeed. There's not a shred of doubt in my mind that you were destined for this."

He paused for a moment before pushing open the door. Nerienda, who had been standing silently on the other side with her ear pressed firmly against it, jumped backward, embarrassed to be caught eavesdropping. Cyneric simply apologized for the run-in and continued on his way with a small, bemused smile.

Nerienda waited only a moment for Cyneric to pass and then rushed into the house.

"What did he say?" she asked. "What did he want?" The two had spoken so softly, she was barely able to make out the whispers.

Judith looked at her maid. She was the only person in the world who knew her better than Cyneric. "He wants me to save the people," she said.

Nerienda looked at her quizzically. "How so?"

"He wants me to travel to Holofernes's camp, win over the lord's trust, and then kill him once I am able to get close enough."

Nerienda let out a gasp. "But…how?"

Judith shook her head. "I don't know, but he has great faith in me. He acts as if it is ordained by God."

"Perhaps it is," Nerienda suggested. "You pray all day and night, and I've never known anyone who has more faith than you. Still, doing this alone is dangerous, not to mention unheard of for a woman."

Nerienda shook her head for a moment as she contemplated sending the girl out alone through the forest and into an army of enemy soldiers whose reputation of brutality preceded them. While she trusted Cyneric's wisdom, she refused to let the maiden take on such a task alone.

"What if I were to go with you?" Nerienda asked cautiously, unsure what the girl would think of such an idea.

Now it was Judith's turn to look shocked. "I don't even know if I'm going myself. Besides, I couldn't let you."

"Of course you could," she interrupted. "We have been together through everything—the death of your mother, the death of your father, illness, famine, siege. We have been together through all of it. No sense stopping now. I am an old woman, and my days are numbered, so let me make the most of them."

Judith gave a slow nod. "It would be nice to have a companion."

"Then you'll do it?" Nerienda asked.

"I haven't said yes yet," Judith responded. "I told Cyneric to give me until morning, and then I would send you to let him know."

Nerienda smiled. "Then I shall leave you with your thoughts. Don't overthink it, though, Judith. Just follow your heart."

Judith left the house and climbed onto the roof. She fell into deep prayer, and that prayer caused her to fall into an even deeper sleep. In her dream, she was surrounded by her father, her mother, Nerienda, Godwine, and all those she loved. They were celebrating with her, and she was carrying a gold crown in her hands. Trumpets were sounding forth a victory call, and crowds of people were falling at her feet. She thought she even recognized Cyneric among them. True, his hair was blond instead of the normal red, and he seemed to stand taller than in real life, but his eyes gave him away. She felt courageous, victorious, peaceful, and loved. Then her father leaned forward and whispered in her ear, "Go. We are with you."

With the trumpet blasts still ringing in her ears, Judith awoke. The sun was just peeking over the horizon, and the answer was obvious. She didn't like the thought of leaving the protection of the town, but it no longer seemed like the choice was hers. Her father had returned from the grave to give her a command, and she was not going to disobey him. It seemed to go against all logic and reason, but she decided she and Nerienda would set out for the enemy camp as soon as possible.

She called the old woman to her, and together they prepared a meal of meager portions with some grain and wilted produce. They did their best to make the food presentable and delicious, adding spices from their small collection to entice the palate. By the time the meal was fully prepared, it was mid-morning, and Judith sent an invitation for Cyneric to join them for supper.

CHAPTER 3

Five months after the Bethulian siege began, Holofernes saw that his thanes were growing restless. Waiting was not something his men were good at, and they were growing weary. They were ready to overtake Bethulia, reap the spoils of war, and return home to their families. Holofernes understood their concerns, but he was a skilled general and knew the virtue of waiting out a blockaded city. Still, something needed to be done. Holofernes knew that if his men could not fight, the next best option was a traditional feast. He called together his advisors along with his right-hand man, Toland. Together they planned out a feast greater than any had ever seen.

The preparations took two weeks, and the soldiers dove into their assignments with renewed vigor and enthusiasm. There was much to be done, and all hands were needed. Because the encampment was temporary, there was no mead hall, so Holofernes assigned a large group of men the task of erecting a tent for their purposes. A smaller group was assigned to make sure the interior was as much like a mead hall as their own at home. The temporary hall needed to be large enough to house every one of the one thousand men in Holofernes's army.

A dozen of the strongest men were assigned to build the three tables that would be needed. Placed in a U shape, the three tables would seat men on each side, bringing with the close proximity a comradery that could be found nowhere else. The twelve men scoured the nearby woods for the biggest, tallest, and sturdiest trees they could find. After carting the trunks back to camp, they began building the tables for the feast.

Bucc, the lone artisan of the twelve, etched carvings of their recent conquests into the tabletops. He carved pictures of battles and towns and the war animals: eagles, ravens, and wolves. He etched a great map into the head table, showing the tracts of land that now belonged to their lord. He carved a great dragon whose tail stretched across all three tables. During a battle with a north-western town close to the Welsh woods, a band of soldiers swore they had seen a great lizard flying through the sky—an omen of their impending victory. Above the central map he placed the seal of his lord: a full-grown buck with twelve points on his antlers. While he slowly progressed down the tables one foot at a time, another man followed behind, applying a coat of beeswax to polish every inch.

In the meantime, Holofernes ordered everyone who had ever stitched a wound or bandage to bring their finest animal skins and construct an extension off the main tent large enough to fit his army under it. The lead doctor of the army was placed in charge of the operation, and he personally saw to it that every added skin was sutured in such a way as to make the whole tent appear seamless. The tawny ceiling covered the large expanse of ground like a great beige cloud. The sides of the tent were left open, both for ventilation and light. Sturdy poles of oak and elm held the new skins in place. When the tent was completed, the awning was a sight to behold, vast and smooth.

Preparations were made outside the tent as well. Those who lacked artistic skill were sent out to collect firewood. A dozen bonfires were to be set ablaze just before the feast began, and large piles of wood were needed to keep them going long into the night. Logs were stacked high, and every effort was made to keep the wood as dry as possible. Furthermore, pits were dug to control and maintain the fires no matter how long the feast lasted.

Holofernes gave his cooks straightforward instructions to create a meal so delicious that no feast would ever taste as good as the food that night. The instructions were simple, but the men in charge of the meal spent their days perspiring in fear. Slaughtering and butchering the large number of animals needed to feed the masses was no easy feat. Heated arguments ensued over how much salt to add, how long to cook the meat, and which bread recipe to use. It was finally decided, after a broken nose and three chipped teeth, that the men would make two types of bread using two different recipes. They hoped Holofernes would see the variety as a novelty and not a failed attempt at compromise.

The fights that arose over the food preparations, though, were nothing compared to the arguments that occurred over the mead. While on the warpath, Holofernes and his men managed to amass a sizeable collection of mead, but no one town had mead that tasted like another. Days were spent testing, in excess, the mead of each town. Fists flew as the men argued over which one was best. They finally agreed that the finest mead—well, the finest according to the majority—would be set aside for Holofernes and his closest advisors. The thanes of high rank were given the next best, and so on and so forth. Truthfully, though, the fighting was all for naught, because it would all end up mixed together with brine and spit by the end of the night.

After several weeks, preparations were nearly ready. The last of the tasks were underway, though orders were given to keep the walls of the central tent down until the celebrations began. Holofernes noticed that as the feast day grew closer, his men walked a little taller and whistled a bit more freely. Laughter could be heard again after months of grumbling, and the dispositions of even the biggest curmudgeons were jovial. It was clear that morale was at an all-time high, and it seemed that Holofernes's order for the greatest of feasts might just become a reality.

In the meantime, Holofernes set about the luxurious task of assigning gifts of gold and treasures to his men. He planned to hand out the gifts at the feast, and he spent splendid afternoons poring over his stockpile of loot. Toland followed dutifully behind him, taking notes of who was to be given which gift, all the while curious to see if Holofernes would offer anything to him.

Five days before the feast, on a bright afternoon, Holofernes was going through a heavy bag of armor. He pulled out a tarnished but otherwise nearly perfect helmet with gold and silver plating. He immediately recognized the worth of the object and remembered the old lord who had fallen in battle while wearing it. *Wasn't it Toland who knocked him off his horse and pierced his heart?* he thought to himself. *Yes, it was. I remember seeing his shock of white-blond hair as he stood over the old man.*

"Toland."

"Yes, my lord."

"Wasn't this the helmet of the lord some towns back? The one you had the pleasure of defeating in battle?"

Toland smiled to himself, knowing full well that Holofernes rarely asked a question he did not already know the answer to.

"Yes, my lord. I believe it was. It's a little worse for wear now, but it is the exact same."

"Brilliant," the lord continued. "Have the guards add it to the rest of the pile for polishing. It will be yours before the feast is over."

Toland beamed with pride at the thought of the helmet being his.

Next, Holofernes grabbed the sword of the same old lord. He studied it for a long time. Toland finally interrupted.

"My lord, that sword belonged to the same lord as the helmet you are giving me."

"Of course. I recognized them as a set. Such craftsmanship on it. Truly a work of art. It goes to Knut."

"Yes, my lord, tha—" Toland was forced to bite his tongue. *Knut*, he thought. *Knut had nothing to do with the death of this man. For all we know, he was off taking advantage of some woman in the village. He certainly did that often enough. Why does Knut always get the best of the gifts? He prefers killing people with his bare hands anyway.*

As if he had heard Toland's thoughts, Holofernes said, "Knut is my fiercest warrior. No man is more brutal in war than he is, and as such he must be honored for it. Besides, his sword is abysmal, barely worth the weight it is to carry around." Holofernes laughed to himself. "Sometimes I think he kills men with his bare hands because his sword wouldn't cause even a scratch."

Toland pushed down the anger that had bubbled up at the sound of Knut's name. There was more to war than brute strength: strategy, planning—weren't those the things that won battles? He and Holofernes spent hours each day carefully laying out each attack. By all accounts, the sword should belong to him as well, he had earned it. He swallowed his frustrations and took a deep breath.

"Yes, of course," he said. "I'll just go call the men to take this all away then. We've been at this for some time now. Perhaps we should take a break?"

Holofernes nodded. "Quite right, I think. Send some mead to my tent. Thank you, old friend." Holofernes turned and walked away without waiting for a response.

Toland pursed his lips but did as he was told. He always did as he was told.

CHAPTER 4

Cyneric was unsure what awaited him when he arrived at Judith's home. To his surprise, it appeared that Judith and Nerienda had used up nearly all of their provisions to provide a small feast worthy of a lord's presence. The table was set for three, and he was happy to eat with company.

Though he had refused food the night before, today he graciously sat down and accepted their kindness. Together they prayed over their food and then sat in silence as Nerienda served them. Cyneric was keenly aware that his portion was double in size to either woman's, but again, he humbly accepted the offer without rebuke. Then he waited in the quiet stillness for someone to speak.

After a few minutes, it became apparent that neither woman would utter the first word. So, he carefully finished chewing the bite of bread he had taken and cleared his throat to begin.

"Thank you so much for your hospitality this afternoon. The food is delicious, and I appreciate the time you took to prepare it."

Both women smiled.

"It was nothing. We are always happy to serve our lord," Judith said.

The sentence hung in the air awkwardly. Cyneric finally continued. "Forgive my boldness, but I assume this invitation can only mean that you have come to a decision."

He looked Judith squarely in the face as he spoke, and she knew she couldn't linger over her decision any longer.

"Yes, my lord," she managed to utter. "After careful deliberation and much prayer, I have decided to do as you ask and venture to the enemy camp. But I must insist that Nerienda come with me. She has agreed to make the journey as my attendant. She will not be a liability…only a help, as she has always been. If you agree to this, we can discuss the arrangements that need to be made."

Cyneric let out a long, slow sigh of relief. The heaviness he had felt for the past several months seemed to lift in a moment, and he found himself laughing out loud.

Judith looked at him in alarm, but he only shook his head, still smiling.

"Thank you, Judith," he finally said. Then, with a certainty he didn't even know he had, he continued. "You are the only one who can save us, and I am confident you will return victorious."

Judith gave a meek smile, but it was Nerienda who had the forethought to ask the most important question.

"Do you have a plan in place to get us to the enemy camp, my lord?"

The three talked long into the night. It was clear that Cyneric's plan was well thought out, just the way it should be when a lord sends his thanes into battle. Only this time, it wasn't his men he was sending but the one person in the city he cherished most. He didn't share his darkest thoughts with her, but he knew that if Judith did not return home, the city would most likely fall to ruin. Moreover, his heart would be broken into a thousand pieces. *Perhaps too shattered to ever mend*, he thought as he studied her face in the candlelight.

After everyone clearly understood the plan, Cyneric thanked

the women for the meal and excused himself to go and make the necessary arrangements for their departure the following night. Before he left, he gave Nerienda a great hug of appreciation. The embrace caused her thoughts to dart back to the boy she used to hold in her arms when he and Judith were playmates. He had grown into a man since that time, and she found that she could not envelop him the way she had ten years ago. Still, the warmth of his arms brought an affectionate smile to her face. *I always did find him endearing*, she thought.

Cyneric then took Judith's hand in both of his and looked into her eyes with the deepest gratitude. He held her gaze for just a moment. *She has changed so much,* he thought, *but those eyes are still as wild, mischievous, and beautiful as ever. She has the cunning for this. It's still in her.*

Then he simply whispered, "Thank you."

"You are welcome," Judith replied. "We will see you when we return."

Judith's statement sounded far more reassuring than she actually felt, but to admit there was an alternative to returning home was impossible. She didn't dare let her mind wander to all the other possibilities that could transpire over the course of their journey. Not now. The mere thought of failure would have sent her crumbling to the floor, and she was not about to let Cyneric see her like that... especially if this was to be their last encounter.

Cyneric gave Judith's hand a strong but gentle squeeze, and then he showed himself to the door. He turned around once more to look at the two women. "While you are away, I will never stop praying for you," he said with sincere affection.

As he walked out into the settling dusk, he had only one thought running through his mind. *Come back to me, Judith. No matter what happens, come back to me.*

Judith spent the night praying. Then as morning broke, she arose from her seat in the corner of their home and turned to Nerienda.

"Prepare the bathwater. It is time."

***

Judith stood over the bath, looking puzzled. She rarely bathed as it was, and she certainly wasn't accustomed to seeing rose petals, pink and red, floating delicately on the surface of the water. The entire room was filled with the aroma of the roses and lavender oil that Nerienda had infused in the bathwater. *These must have been left over from Father's travels*, she thought. *Such a strangely familiar smell despite the years since they last filled this house!*

Judith discarded her wool dress and undid her braid so that her long, light-blonde hair fell free, reaching down to the small of her back. Then she dipped her toes in the bath. She was surprised by the warmth of the water. The water she used daily in the bowl on her nightstand was always cold, as was the water for her occasional bathing, but even with the chill lingering in the early morning air, the bath was almost uncomfortably hot.

She sank down into the warm water, letting it wrap itself around her and soak into her coarse skin. For one rare moment, she allowed herself to relax. She breathed in deeply, and the floral scent calmed her.

Her thoughts started to drift freely, and as always, they led her to her childhood. She remembered her father easily. Tall but gentle, he cherished Judith and everything she did. She smiled as she remembered how he loved to laugh, and then she remembered the song, their song, that he'd sing to her whenever she was sad, especially when she cried before he embarked on another one of his trips to the east. *"Time may pass, and life moves on, but my love for you remains. Take comfort in that and you will know my love in every age."*

As the song in her heart repeated itself, happy memories flooded her mind. But in an instant the familiar vision and voice changed. Cyneric filled her mind—his face, first as a child and then as a man. Memories of their early days together played through her mind. Then he started singing her song. The longing for her friend fanned the spark of love she still held for him, but as she felt it grow, she was reminded of his recent visits and the task before her. The peace she felt was replaced by fear.

Her eyes snapped open and her whole body shivered. Fear ran through her veins. Quickly, she grabbed the piece of pumice Nerienda had left close by and started to scrub every inch of herself; her arms, legs, fingers, toes, abdomen, nothing was spared. She ended up scouring her legs red and raw in a futile attempt to rid her mind of her worries.

After she finished bathing and stepped out of the tub, she called for Nerienda, who soaked her hair and slathered perfumed oil on it. The oils gave Judith's hair, which had been dull from neglect, a sheen that rivaled a queen's. Then Nerienda took a fine comb made of shell and brushed her hair until it was dry. Every time she brought the comb to the top of Judith's head, she gently gave it a tug and worked it through the tangles. Then she pulled the teeth down Judith's back to the end of her long locks just above the girl's waist.

Judith's hair was gold, as pale and light as the driest straw, and after Nerienda finished, it had the softness and shine of pure silk. Once the hair was dry, Nerienda braided it, as was customary of the time. She selected a golden cord and set the thick band high on Judith's forehead in a regal fashion before working it into the intricate plaiting. When she was done, she stepped back to view her work and gave a nod of approval.

"There you go. Beautiful hair for a beautiful girl," she said.

Judith blushed at the words. She wasn't accustomed to receiving compliments. Still, when Nerienda handed her a mirror and swept the long braid across her shoulder so she could get a better look, Judith had to agree that her hair had never looked, smelled, or felt quite so beautiful.

Though she'd bathed and had her hair plaited, Judith was not even halfway finished with her preparations. Nerienda followed her to a small table by the bed. In all the years since her father's passing, Nerienda had not seen the girl reach for anything on the table.

Carefully, Judith picked up an ornate box and gingerly opened it to reveal the small containers of make-up inside. The whole collection, box included, was one of the last gifts her father had given her. It was said to have come from a far-off place called Africa. The merchants told Deorwine of the mythical creatures that lived there, and they described the brave warriors who hunted these creatures that were so big ten strong men could not lift them. The box had been made from the largest of these beasts, the elephant. The entire container was carved from ivory, and from the carving on the lid an elephant stared back at the viewer with its big ears, elongated snout, and ivory tusks on full display.

When Deorwine gave her the box, Judith had been more stunned by the beauty of the container than by the make-up, and she had carefully placed the gift by her bedside. She had planned to save the powders and creams for a special occasion, perhaps her wedding. However, after her father died, she had all but forgotten about the little box and the luxuries held inside.

Judith sat in the candlelight, admiring the container, but Nerienda could see something was keeping her mistress from continuing her preparations. She took a few steps closer and saw that Judith had tears streaming down her pale cheeks. She was fumbling with the make-up containers, unsure how to properly apply them. Catching sight of the setting sun, Nerienda knew they were running short on time. She knelt down next to her young mistress and placed her own wrinkled hands on Judith's delicate ones, stilling the shaking. Judith looked into the old woman's eyes.

"I am so afraid."

Nerienda's weary eyes crinkled and a warm smile crossed her face.

"Cyneric would not have asked you if he didn't think you could carry out the orders. Judith, you may not know it, but you have far more courage than any woman I know. Never once did I see you afraid of thunder, the forest, or the strange men and beasts your father spoke of. And on top of that, you have the faith of a saint. You know, few people in life are lucky enough to fulfill their destiny, and even fewer have the privilege of recognizing it as it happens. I think this plan is exactly where your destiny lies."

With a reassuring squeeze of her hands, Judith breathed a deep sigh.

Nerienda opened the ivory box and began applying the make-up. She smudged the thick, black powder around Judith's eyes and then applied a silver-colored one to her lids. Judith's already light-blue eyes now looked like the perfect spring sky. Next, Nerienda added rose powder to each cheekbone, giving Judith's thin face a healthy fullness. Finally, Nerienda mixed a touch of bathwater with a deep cherry-colored powder, creating a paste, and added it to Judith's lips. As Nerienda stepped back to inspect her work, she sucked in her breath. She scarcely recognized the woman before her. Judith's beauty had never been more evident.

Nerienda then began helping Judith change into the outfit they had laid out for her the night before. After careful deliberation, they decided on a royal-blue linen dress with a gold hem; the dress came to just above her knees in an elegant curve. It had a fitted bodice and was gathered at the waist with a leather belt. An emerald-green skirt reaching the ground was placed underneath it. On her head Judith wore a light-blue veil, which fully covered her blonde hair and gold headband. Apart from a few curls that refused to be tamed and peered out of the veil, the look was flawless.

Nerienda laced delicate silver slippers on Judith's feet, another gift from her father. The shoes reflected the candlelight as the shadows deepened outside. Nearly done with her preparations, Judith walked back over to the small table that held her make-up. There was another ornate box, carved from cedar, that sat beside her ivory one. The box had an aroma that filled the space around it with a sweet, fresh woody scent. From this box, Judith began to remove her jewelry.

She chose three gold rings and two necklaces: one silver with sea glass, the other copper with garnets. On her arms she placed five bangles of pressed gold, silver, and bright copper. Her earrings were saltwater pearls gifted to her by her father. Last but not least, she readjusted the small, simple necklace she was already wearing. Her most prized possession. It was a small wooden carving of a bird, which hung suspended by a string short enough to rest on her collarbone. This little bird was the very first piece of jewelry her father had ever given her.

Shortly after Judith's mother died, Deorwine decided his infant daughter needed something to remember her by. He carved a small bird out of the wood scraps he had on hand. This bird was an exact replica of a necklace Judith's grandfather had given her mother when she was young. Deorwine's wife loved the necklace so much she never took it off, and he decided it was right for her to be buried with it. Still, he wanted his daughter to have a connection to the woman who had carried her for nine months, so he spent hours carving the bird from memory. Then he carefully strung the little creature on a piece of strong cord and kept it safely hidden by his bed.

When Judith was three years old, he decided she was old enough to have a necklace. On her third birthday, Deorwine brought out the little bird and carefully placed it around Judith's neck. He spent the night telling his sweet young girl all about her mother and how she and Judith were the only two women in the world who had ever worn this necklace. Despite her young age, Judith vowed to treasure the gift forever. Though she never felt a true connection to her mother—she'd hemorrhaged so quickly after Judith was born that she never even got a chance to hold her—Judith loved the gift because her father, her favorite person in the entire world, had made it for her. No matter how old she grew, she was always able to remember the night he gave it to her and the stories he told of a woman who looked just like her and loved her so much that she used her last breath to bring her safely into the world.

Once every last piece of jewelry was securely in place, Nerienda stepped back to admire Judith. She seemed to be radiating a heavenly light from within her. Anyone looking at her in that moment would have thought she had supernatural powers, the ability to move the constellations in the sky or summon roses to bloom in winter.

Surely, Nerienda thought, *this can't be the same woman who dresses in coarse fabrics and sleeps on a mat of reeds.* And yet, she knew it could be no one else.

"You are nearly ready, my dear," she said as she walked across the room to fetch the heavy cloak Judith would need for the dangerous journey ahead. The warm wool cloak was a dark gray and fastened with a sturdy metal buckle—the same one that had hung on Deorwine's belt for decades. After his death, it had been repurposed as the cloak's clasp.

Judith lifted the hood around her head and slipped sturdy leather shoes on over her silver slippers. She was ready. With her outerwear in place, her beauty was hidden—exactly as they had intended. Walking out of the city limits and traversing the several miles of wooded terrain was something that needed to be done with stealth. The less attention she drew, the better.

While Nerienda quickly gathered their provisions and her own cloak, Judith prayed one final, fervent prayer for their success and safety. Then, trembling with cold and fear, she took Nerienda's warm and steady hand, and the two departed into the night.

CHAPTER 5

Silently closing the door to the cottage behind them, Judith and Nerienda tiptoed out into the night with only the moon as their guide. The familiar, friendly streets looked ominous and foreboding in the darkness. Even with the cover of night, they hid in the shadows, walking swiftly but silently. Candlelight and glowing embers showed from the windows of the houses they passed. Inside they could see families huddled together, trying to keep warm against the autumn chill.

When they passed Ellette's home, Judith saw the child curled up on her father's lap. She appeared to be sleeping, wrapped snugly in a thick blanket. The girl had always been small for her age, but when her father, one of Cyneric's largest thanes, held her, the child's withering frame was alarmingly evident. Judith found herself praying as they darted from shadow to shadow. *If you can only save one in this city, Lord, please let it be her.*

It did not take long to reach the blacksmith's hut, just on the perimeter within the city walls. Cyneric instructed them to go to Bronson's home so that the iron bender could lead them out of the city, where they were to meet Olaf, the huntsman who would take them the rest of the journey to the enemy camp. Only four people knew of Judith's mission: Cyneric, Bronson, Olaf, and the head guard.

The gate to the city had remained closed for months. No man, woman, child, or animal had entered or exited the city through the gates in that time. Opening the giant doors for Judith in the middle of the night would quickly arouse suspicion with townspeople or any scout from Holofernes's camp who happened to be watching from a distance. So, Judith was to depart from a side entrance only a handful of people knew about.

This small, secret entrance was the only way the townspeople had been able to survive. Early in the morning before the village awoke, farmers from the surrounding area would bring what little they had to the town by way of the hidden entrance. Now, even the farmers were running out of food. Those farms that hadn't been burned to the ground or destroyed in pillaging were forced to give over what they had to the enemy camp.

Judith tapped lightly on the blacksmith's door. Before her second knock, the door quickly swung open and the women were ushered inside. The one-room home was small but warm, and the dim candlelight from the lone flickering flame cast large shadows on the walls.

"Do you have everything you need?" Bronson asked in a hushed whisper as he silently closed the door behind them.

"We do," Judith responded quietly.

"Food, cloaks, weapons?"

"No weapons," Judith said. "We were instructed against them. Instead, we have poisonous berries brewed in a tea. They are potent enough to kill a bear."

The smith gave a slight smirk. "If you can get the bear to drink it," he murmured.

Judith pretended not to hear him. She knew the dangers she was walking into and didn't need to be reminded of them. Truth be told, she and Nerienda didn't even have poisonous berries. All they carried with them was a few days' ration of food and the small containers of make-up and perfume. Cyneric had insisted she bring no weapons of any kind. If she were caught with one, it would surely raise suspicion about her intentions. Therefore, she was to use the weapons she would find at the camp. They knew there would not be a short supply of them.

With barely a sound, the blacksmith pressed something smooth and cold into her hand. The chill of the object gave her a start, and when she looked down, she could just make out the outline of a small dagger. As she held it up, a glint of light bounced off the metal, and she saw the craftsmanship that had gone into making it.

"It's not much," Bronson said. "Still, a woman going into an army camp ought to have some protection."

Judith reached out for the blacksmith's hand and squeezed it gently. "Thank you," she whispered. "But…" before she could protest any further, Bronson interrupted.

"No buts. I insist."

Judith nodded her consent. After a long silence, Bronson cleared his throat.

"We better get moving. The entrance isn't easy to find at night, even for me… even though it's on my property. Lord Godwine, and now Lord Cyneric, have always paid me a small price for keeping guard against the town's secret entrance."

Bronson led them through the smith shop attached to his hut and out a back opening. They walked a fair distance before they ran right into the city wall.

"It should be just a little to the right now. Not too far, though. I have a direct sightline to it during the day from my shop. Too far right and I couldn't see it."

Judith followed with Nerienda close behind her. It certainly made sense to have the smith on guard. The day-to-day work of hammering out weapons and tools for the city's guards and tradesmen could only be done by someone with strong arms and stamina. As she watched the smith's intimidating silhouette walk in front of her, it was clear he could handle himself in a fight. They finally stopped at a spot that was particularly overgrown. In the clear moonlight, Judith could see the tall grass and shrubs reaching just high enough to touch the full, low-hanging tree branches.

Bronson parted the grasses and lifted a few small branches. There they found a small opening in the wall. A bowed log left just enough space for a grown man to squeeze in or out. The smith gave a soft dove's coo, and an owl's hoot immediately echoed through the opening.

"Olaf is waiting for you. Go now. Remember to go to the main gate when you return."

Judith looked up at Bronson. She carefully studied his kind face, knowing it might be the last one she would see in Bethulia if the journey didn't go as planned. Although the town was not always the most comforting or welcoming place, it was the only home she knew, and she wanted to remember it, no matter what lay ahead.

Sensing her anxiety, Bronson broadened his gentle smile and said, "Godspeed. I will see you when you return." He held out his hands to assist the women through the wall. He gave Judith's arm a gentle nudge of encouragement as she stepped into the opening and took the few quick steps to get to the other side.

As Judith crossed through the four feet of splintered tree trunk, her veil got caught on a wooden shard, tearing at the bottom. She nearly fell but stumbled forward just far enough for two strong hands to lift her up and onto solid ground.

"Thank you," she said, without catching a glimpse of the stranger. He'd no sooner set her down than he turned back to the wall to help Nerienda, who was slightly encumbered with the bag of provisions.

Both Judith and Nerienda felt a chill run down their spines as the huntsman turned to face them. Olaf was nothing like Bronson. He was a beastly man, completely clothed in animal furs. He had thick, unkempt facial hair covering every feature but his coal-black eyes, which were constantly darting from one corner of the forest to another. He did not say a word or even look at the women. Instead, he simply walked past them into the thick of the forest, leaving Judith and Nerienda to follow him.

Olaf moved quickly and stealthily, keeping himself and the women veiled in the shadows. He seemed to know exactly where to place each step to avoid brambles and tree roots. Judith and Nerienda followed as best they could, though they could not match Olaf's long strides. Occasionally, their guide would stop to examine an opening in the tree canopy, and he'd look up to study the stars above him. Then just as abruptly as he'd halted their journey, he would begin again.

They continued for hours, walking up hills, over tree stumps, around fallen logs, and through dense thickets. Finally, they came to a large clearing. It was a beautiful, tranquil place filled with flowers that bloomed at night.

Olaf turned to look at the women for the first time all night. He motioned for them to stay where they were then slipped silently back into the woods, leaving Judith and Nerienda alone in the open clearing. Time seemed to creep by for Judith. As she stood in the meadow, the stillness of the night enveloped her. Her anxieties hummed in her ears. Though she stood in an open space, Judith felt crushed by her fear.

The moon shone brightly, casting a luminescence on the flowers at Judith's feet, but she could not see their ethereal beauty. Instead, she felt herself slowly crumbling toward the ground and was about to let out a scream when a hand quickly covered her mouth.

Nerienda had seen her distress. As the young woman began moaning in terror, Nerienda covered Judith's mouth. They could not afford to give away their position now; not when they were so close.

Surprised by the hand, Judith snapped back to reality. Still trembling, she collapsed into Nerienda's arms. The cold stillness that hid them felt deafening, and the owl's spectral call sent a chill down her spine.

When Judith was a child, her father told stories of the forest, stories designed to keep children from venturing into the woods on their own. The fate that awaited one who got lost there was dire. The fairy tales told of a dangerous place inhabited by evil beings. Ghosts, witches, sorcerers: they all lived there. Perhaps even more threatening were the wolves, ravens, and eagles that made their home in the forest and only ventured out when they sensed a battle looming. Fresh kill and wounded men were easy targets. Like most children, Judith and Cyneric had played along the forest's edge, never daring to set foot more than a few inches into it.

In only a few hours' time, Judith had already traveled further into the forest than most, and her father's words echoed in her mind. "The woods," Deorwine would say, "are thick with trees and the dangers that live among them. They are not a place for a young girl. Only the most dangerous and disloyal men can be found there."

When a thane deserted, dishonored his lord by running from battle, or performed some inexcusable wrongdoing, he was cast out of the community, destined to wander through the woods for life… a fate worse than death. Other might be banished from their homes, too, if they were found to have committed a treasonous crime. Desertion of one's community for any reason was inexcusable. Rarely did another community take in an outcast. Instead, he lived alone, forced to defend himself against the dangers found in the forest.

Now, wrapped in the darkness of the woods, Judith thought only of the rumors of the army they were headed toward. She knew Holofernes was not like other men. He was a Celt, and his army did not act honorably as other armies did. In the months that Bethulia had been under siege, gossip ran rampant that Holofernes's men weren't men at all but monsters who took human form only when they were to defeat a new enemy. Even though Cyneric had reassured her that Holofernes and his men were mere mortals, now the thought made her shiver. She felt alone and defenseless in the meadow. Even as Nerienda held her in her arms, she was frightened and could not begin to fathom the perils that awaited them.

CHAPTER 6

A twig snapped, causing Judith to jump. She saw Olaf emerging from the woods. Standing at the tree line, he silently beckoned the women closer to him. When they reached him, he spoke for the first time.

"There is a hill up ahead that we must climb over. There is a family of wolves who live at the base of it, so be careful as you go. Do not disturb the parents or the pups. They could give you more trouble than the whole army you were sent to defeat. Once we are safely over the hill, we must cross a wide stream. The current is swift, and the water is cold, but it's the sharp rocks that can really hurt you. Tread lightly and test each step before putting weight on it. Once we reach the other side, our path gets easier. Fewer trees, flatter ground. We will be at the camp before the sun rises."

Nerienda nodded in understanding, but Judith continued her trance-like stare. Olaf made a move to continue their journey, but Nerienda stopped him.

"Will you give us a moment?" she asked.

Olaf looked at her in annoyance and was about to object, but after another quick glance at Judith, he relented. *The poor girl must be more scared than she's ever been in her life*, he thought.

When he had heard of Cyneric's plan, he agreed to his part, but secretly he was outraged. He felt that Judith's role in this scheme was nothing more than a cruel death sentence. If Judith failed, which Olaf thought was likely, and Holofernes learned of her plan, his army would waste no time in pillaging the city.

Nerienda led Judith back into the open meadow so the light of the moon would allow them a clear picture of each other.

"Judith," Nerienda began firmly but softly, but her young mistress offered no response. Nerienda grabbed the maiden's shoulders and shook her, calling her name again. Judith blinked sharply and looked at Nerienda as if she had been suddenly awakened from a troubled dream. She let out a startled gasp as she tried to refocus on Nerienda's face.

Nerienda relaxed her grip, but she kept her hands on Judith's shoulders. "I know you are frightened, but you must be brave," she said. "I know the forest is terrifying. But understand that what we are about to do, the place we are going, the men we will be dealing with, they are the real threat… not the stories you heard of the forest when you were a child. You must compose yourself. If you can't get yourself together now, you will fail at your task before it has even begun."

Judith looked at Nerienda, tearful. "How can I be brave when there is so much fear inside me?" she whispered.

Nerienda suddenly felt an overwhelming sense of compassion.

"When someone is forced into a fearful situation, there are always two options. You can choose to retreat, or you can choose to fight. Retreat always ends in defeat, but when you choose to fight, there is a chance, no matter how small, for victory. You must cast aside fear and doubt and know that if you choose to fight, you will not be alone. A good lord always goes into battle with his thanes, and your Lord will be with you."

Judith took a deep breath, silently prayed for guidance and courage, and then blessed herself with the sign of her God. Still shaking, she took Nerienda's arm. The two women turned and walked back to Olaf. When they reached him, he gave a slight nod to Nerienda and began leading the small party, again, through the forest.

The march up the hill was challenging, and the women had to stop twice to rest. As they neared the top, a wolf let out a long howl nearby. Olaf stopped dead in his tracks, causing the women to bump into him. "They know we are here," he whispered.

The howling continued for several minutes and other wolves began to join in, their voices carrying from the far corners of the forest. Finally, silence returned. Olaf waited a few more moments before continuing across the rugged terrain.

Once they were over the hilltop, they quickened their pace and found themselves at the bank of the stream in no time. Olaf led the way, crossing with ease. He stood on the other side and waited impatiently for his followers to catch up.

The women took off their shoes, and Nerienda carried them in one hand with their bag in the other. Then they took their first step into the fast-flowing, chilly water, but before they had even found a steady rock to support their weight, they heard a low growl behind them.

Turning, Judith found herself standing mere feet from a large gray wolf. The hair on the back of its neck was standing straight up as it lowered its head toward the ground, ready to spring forward. The animal was so close, Judith could see its hot breath in the cool night air. The beast gnashed its teeth as its eyes flashed yellow in the moonlight, and another low, menacing growl rolled off its tongue.

Neither woman moved until Judith, finding her bearings, whispered. "Go, Nerienda. Get across the river quickly."

Nerienda began to object. "Judith, I can't leave you here…"

Judith cut her off. "Go," she hissed, "that's an order."

Judith had never once ordered her to do anything. She was always polite, always kind when making a request. Nerienda was too stunned by Judith's boldness to object further, so she turned and began crossing the stream cautiously, leaving her mistress alone with the wolf.

Judith could hear the splish-splash of Nerienda's steps as the old woman waded through the water. When Nerienda was safely on the other side, Judith turned her attention back to the ferocious beast in front of her. She locked eyes with the animal and steadied her breathing. Suddenly, all her thoughts stopped. Her mind cleared and she found herself reacting based on the lessons she'd learned from Cyneric when they were children, just as he had predicted. Her fear was replaced by intuition and action.

Judith crouched low to the ground, and keeping her movements slow and steady, she drew her new dagger from her belt. Then she held it out in front of her in a fighting stance. The moonlight glistened off the blade, and the flash made the wolf even angrier. For one brief moment, Judith's hands and knees trembled, but she steadied herself as she pushed her fear aside.

Judith and the wolf continued to stare at each other, neither one moving. Judith took a step further into the stream, ready to wade through the water backward, but as she did so, she slipped on a loose rock. She caught herself, but the commotion caused a small splash. The wolf, startled by the sound, lunged toward her. Her first instinct was to shut her eyes and recoil, bracing for the attack, but then she remembered where she was and what she was doing. She remembered who she was fighting for.

Her eyes snapped opened, focused, and narrowed. The wolf began to run forward. She quickly jumped back onto solid ground, calculated the beast's steps, waited only a moment, then lunged and thrust the dagger deep into the top of the animal's head.

Despite the hard bone of the wolf's skull, the knife crushed it in one blow. Judith was bathed in a shower of blood, the spray hitting her face. She watched as the animal collapsed to the ground. She scanned it for any sign of life, but the beast lay dead.

Stepping on the wolf's snout for leverage, Judith pulled the dagger out of its head. It took more strength to remove it than it had to sink it into the animal's flesh and bone. As she pulled the knife away, she noticed her cloak was spattered with blood and her hands and bare feet were colored red. *I killed a living creature*, she thought. Tears started streaming down her face, but she knew she had to get going. She quickly crossed the stream. Once on the other side, she fell weakly into Nerienda's open arms.

"Well done, Judith," she whispered into the girl's veil. "You handled that beautifully."

Judith looked up into Nerienda's face. In the moonlight, she could make out every feature and wrinkle on the old woman's face. She also saw her warm eyes shining brightly. There was a glint of happiness and pride in them.

"I was so scared," Judith cried.

"Hush now," Nerienda said as she dried the girl's tears. "You were very brave. Always remember this moment and call forth that strength and courage when you find yourself in danger."

Judith stood, took a deep breath, and nodded in understanding.

"Let's get you cleaned up. Give me your cloak, Judith," she continued. "There is blood all over it, and I need to get it out. You can't show up on the enemy's doorstep with a clear display of what you are capable of."

Nerienda helped Judith slip off her cloak. Then she took it over to the stream, picked up a pumice stone and began to scrub vigorously. It took some time to get all the blood out, but if anyone could remove such a stain, it was Nerienda.

Judith followed her and crouched down to clean her dagger. She dried it on a clean spot on her dress and put it back in her belt. She took a red scarf hidden under her dress and scrubbed her hands and feet until they were clean. Finally, she rinsed the scarf and dabbed it across her face, careful not to smudge her make-up.

As Olaf watched the women work, he whispered as much to himself as anyone else, "There may be hope for Bethulia."

***

Olaf was true to his word. The remainder of the journey was quick and easy compared to what they had been through. They covered a great deal of ground in very little time. At long last, Olaf stopped. It had been hours since he had spoken to the women, but now he turned to them to give his final instructions.

"As soon as you climb this hill, you will be able to see the whole enemy camp. They always wake at first light. Survey the area, and once you feel you know the layout well enough, walk down closer to the camp. But be sure to conceal yourselves until daylight. Then... follow your plan."

Before the women had time to reply, Olaf walked into a densely forested part of the woods, rounded a large tree, and disappeared from view.

The women looked at each other. They had made it through the forest, but the real challenge was just about to begin. They quickly reached the top of the hill where they could see the whole camp. They sat down to rest for the first time all night, and Judith laid her damp cloak flat on the ground to finish drying. They ate an early breakfast of bread and cheese, which Nerienda had carefully packed in their bag.

They discussed the camp over their meal. It seemed that the largest, most important tents were at the center and were protected on all sides by a circle of smaller tents at least ten deep. They made notes of which areas had guards and saw a route that would lead them out of camp once their task was complete.

With their breakfast finished and the layout of the camp memorized, the two women walked down the hill to wait for dawn.

CHAPTER 7

The sun's rays were beginning to peek over the hill, and light spread into the enemy camp, illuminating every corner of the valley. Judith and Nerienda had allowed themselves only a short rest before gingerly making their way down to the base of Holofernes's camp. While considering their options, they watched two sleeping guards.

The two thanes, Acwel and Aart, had been on watch, guarding the edge of the dark forest all night. There had been no threat to the camp in weeks, and dawn found the men sitting on a fallen tree trunk, their backs propped against each other. Their heads softly bobbed and nodded up and down with their synchronized snoring. In their hands they clutched empty mead cups, inadvertently turned upside down as they slept. Dark pools of wet earth appeared at the men's feet where the drinks soaked into the dirt. Though on guard, their belts and battle axes lay on the ground a few feet away, and their swords perched precariously across each man's lap. They were dressed in thick woolen shirts and pants, and each wore a fur hat and cloak to shield against the chilly night air. Their boots, fashioned out of fur, wrapped snugly around their legs up to their knees.

The men slept soundly as the sun continued to rise higher into the sky. The orange, red, and pink colors of dawn had nearly faded when the sharp snap of a twig echoed through the woods.

"Aart, did you hear something?" Acwel sputtered as his eyes snapped open, frantically scanning the forest border for signs of danger.

Aart gave one final snort before rubbing the sleep out of his eyes. Annoyed at being woken up, he grumbled, "I'm sure it was nothing more than a deer or a rabbit. Wait for Bryce and Camden to arrive. They should be starting watch any minute now. Let them figure it out."

Acwel gave a soft admonishment to his fellow guardsman. "It could be a deer, but if it is a wolf, we don't want it prowling so close to camp. We'd better go have a look." He stood up, repositioned his belt, and grabbed his battle axe. Standing motionless for a moment, he cocked his head to one side, watching and listening. After a short moment, he slowly stepped forward, ready to tear down whatever beast challenged him.

As Acwel neared the tree line, Judith and Nerienda held their breath and silently sank low to the ground. It had been Judith's careless step that had caused the twig to break. The snap echoed through the quiet pre-dawn air and sent fear coursing through her veins. She crouched completely motionless, except for the beads of sweat running down her back.

Acwel continued toward them. Assuming the noise had been a rabbit or deer, he crept cautiously. Any sort of fresh meat would make for a delicious breakfast.

He inched closer and began looking through the bushes. Judith and Nerienda could hear his sword hit against his belt buckle. The clinking sound gave away his position. Then they saw his boots as his heavy, muffled steps marched past them. He moved along the forest's edge, and the women could hear his steps fading.

They'd planned to arrive at camp at midday and make an entrance by walking up to the guards and asking for help. Being discovered hiding in the bushes would make the guards suspicious that they were up to something sinister.

Just as they were beginning to breathe a little easier, the sound of the clinking sword grew closer once more. The women held their breath as the pair of shoes came to a stop directly in front of the bush that was concealing them.

Slowly, Judith looked up. The guard's beady eyes stared back at her.

"Well, well, well, what do we have here? Aart, you'd better come look at this."

Before the second guard had time to respond, Judith sprang into action. She jumped up and fearlessly threw her arms around Acwel.

"Oh, thank you, my lord. We are safe now," she cried over Acwel's shoulder. "Sir, we have been running from a monster for five nights with nothing more than the moon to guide us, and we are exhausted. We gave up hope when my dear maid twisted her ankle and could not go on. We took cover here, not knowing where we were and praying that a kind, brave soul would find and rescue us."

Nerienda could hardly believe the scene she was witnessing. Only moments before, Judith had been a timid, terrified girl. Now she was acting as a courageous heroine, and all without any preplanning. When she saw the guard standing over them, she was certain her life was about to come to a swift and bloody end. Judith's quick thinking surprised her, so much so that she caught herself staring at the scene with her mouth agape. Once Judith's story had registered, though, she quickly changed her expression, assumed a look of pain, and grabbed her ankle.

Judith backed away from the dirty guard, lowered her wool hood, and peered sweetly at him.

Acwel stood in stunned silence. He could not believe what was happening. For weeks he and Aart had kept guard at their nightly post without so much as a fox wandering past. Now before him was the most beautiful woman he had ever seen. All his years of training and service could never have prepared him for this.

Acwel knelt to the ground on one knee as he spoke. "My dear lady, who are you running from? Only speak his name, and I will search the entire forest until I find and behead him."

Thinking quickly, Judith gave a warm smile. "How kind of you, good sir. But I am afraid the man chasing us is long gone. We only seek shelter and care for Nerienda's ankle. Is there anyone here who can provide this?"

Acwel looked to Aart, and the two men nodded in agreement. No woman would willingly walk into an army camp of one thousand men if she did not desperately need assistance. Furthermore, the guards gathered that the women must have traveled a far distance since they seemed so ignorant of their army's reputation.

Acwel held out his hand to Judith. "My lady," he began. "I am no lord, only a loyal thane. But you have sought shelter in the camp of the most noble of lords. Aart, help the old woman up and take her to the doctor. And I will care for you, my dear…" his voice hung in the air, fishing for a name.

"Judith. I am Judith," she replied.

"Please, come with me to see my lord, Judith. He will take you in and shield you from your enemies."

Aart begrudgingly walked over to the old woman, knelt down, and carefully gathered Nerienda in his arms. Judith caught

Nerienda's look of worry. Instead of meeting Holofernes together, it seemed they were bound for opposite ends of the camp, not knowing what was to become of the other.

Acwel noticed Nerienda's worried expression too. "Don't worry, old woman," he said through a smile. "The doctor will take good care of you. You and Judith will be back together again by noon."

Judith watched Aart and Nerienda until they were lost in a sea of tents. Then she turned to Acwel, placed her hand in his and followed him through the maze to the center of the camp.

The morning sun had fully risen by this time. Though dew still lingered on the grass, the camp was coming alive. Acwel led Judith amongst the tents, and she tried desperately to position herself within the map she had committed to memory only an hour before. However, she quickly realized the layout was far more haphazard than it had appeared from above, and the distractions around her made concentration difficult. Horses stomped and whinnied, ready for breakfast and a chance to stretch their legs. Soldiers crawled out of tents, yawning, scratching, stretching, and grunting. It did not take long before Judith was completely overwhelmed and lost.

The deeper Acwel led her into the camp, the more quickly news spread of the mysterious and beautiful maiden's arrival. The men stopped their morning routine, quieted, and stood staring at her as she passed, completely in awe of her beauty. She, in turn, did her best to keep her head down, but it wasn't easy. After nearly walking into a tent and then stumbling into the flank of a horse, Judith gave up and raised her eyes.

The men around her seemed to be barbarians in every sense of the word, but to her relief, they were at least human. From what she could tell, no monsters resided here. However, the soldiers' behavior was far from gentle. Their unruly beards and matted hair framed their lustful eyes and open mouths. Wet, pink tongues hung out of their mouths as they stood around licking their lips. Judith shuddered as she passed a man who called to her.

"Beautiful maiden, stay with us. Our lord has plenty of women back home, but we could make use of your company now."

The men around them immediately broke into laughter followed by shouts and grunts of agreement.

Acwel stopped and spoke. "Putnam! That is no way to treat a guest. This lovely woman has been running all night. She fears for her life and seeks safety. Behave yourself."

Then turning back to Judith he said, "Forgive them. We have been away from home for years and have not had a proper woman among us in all that time. Your striking beauty has stirred up their passions, but do not be afraid."

Then speaking loudly for all to hear, "No man will harm you while you are with us. Our lord insists that all visitors be welcomed warmly to our camp." Glaring at Putnam and the other men, Acwel took Judith's hand and led her deeper into the heart of the camp.

As they neared the camp's center, the sweet aroma of mead filled the air and mixed with the scent of rabbit and squirrel that the men had roasted for breakfast over open campfires. With breakfast concluded, many of the men started training. Judith saw swords clash and heard horse hoofs thunder around the camp. The grunts and groans of pinned wrestlers carried far.

In only a matter of moments, the quiet, seemingly deserted camp they had been watching from above teemed with life. A small flock of sheep ran in front of Acwel and Judith just as they were approaching the largest tent. Judith recognized the shelter as the one directly in the camp's center and was thankful to finally have a landmark she remembered. Two guards stood watch on either side of the tent's opening, and as Judith studied her surroundings more closely, she noticed that the tawny animal skins of this tent seemed far superior to those she had just passed.

The soldiers' tents were smaller, with various colored animal skins haphazardly stitched together or laid across each other. However, this center tent was made of large skins, perfectly matched in color and stitched together in an expertly organized pattern. The tent was large, at least ten times the size of the tents the soldiers slept in.

Acwel stopped before the tent's opening and looked to the guard on the right. "Rinan, is our lord within?"

Rinan nodded and asked, "What business do you have with him so early in the morning?" Of course, both guards already knew the nature of his visit. The rumor of a beautiful, fairy-like woman had already reached the guards' ears, and it only took one glance at Judith to confirm the truth of the tale. The guards eyed her with suspicion while secretly admiring her radiance.

Rinan was an average man, neither tall nor short, with ashen skin and light-brown hair. The other guard, Knut, on the other hand, looked the part of a true warrior. He stood nearly as tall as the tent with a muscular frame and fair face. His eyes were pale blue, and his hair was the blondest blonde, almost white. His stare felt more threatening than even the wolf's she'd faced the night before. *He knows why I'm here*, Judith thought and felt her knees buckle, but Knut broke his stare and turned back to watch the surrounding morning regiments. At the same moment, Acwel turned to Judith.

"Come, my lady, enter with me and meet our benevolent leader, the truest of ring bearers."

Rinan and Knut each gave a curt nod of approval. Then Knut, still silent, untied the tent's opening and gestured for them to enter.

CHAPTER 8

The tent was cool and dark, except for a few candles burning somewhere near the center. As Acwel and Judith drew closer toward the dim light, she could see a large man hunched over a table and surrounded by candlelight. The man was holding the candle and gesturing with it as he reviewed an extensive map. His advisor, a tall, lanky man, stood next to the lord, bending low over the map. Their muffled whispers carried only a few feet around them.

Acwel stopped ten paces away from the men, and Judith paused as well, hiding in Acwel's dark shadow.

"Who is there?" the seated man demanded.

"My lord," Acwel began. He stared down at the ground and shifted his feet uneasily. "I am sorry to disturb you, but some strange events occurred this morning that need your attention."

The man at the desk stood, revealing his full height and size. Judith could barely make the figure out in the dark, but what she saw caused her to gasp. He towered over her and the others. He stood nearly seven feet tall and had the girth of an ox. While Anglo-Saxons were traditionally light-skinned and pale, with light hair and blue eyes, this man's hair was jet black. His features were pronounced, and his skin was an olive tone. His eyes were dark and terrifying as they pierced through the shadows of the tent.

Judith felt terror course through her. *What have I gotten myself into?* she thought. *How am I supposed to kill this giant?*

"What matter could be so important as to interrupt my war plans?" the large man growled.

Acwel bowed and began his story. "As I was nearing the end of my watch this morning, I happened upon a young maiden and her maid. They had been traveling all night to escape an evil man, but after the maid hurt her ankle, they could run no further and hid in a thicket not far from our camp. While on guard, I heard a twig snap. Thinking it might be a rabbit for breakfast, I went to investigate. However, instead of an animal, I found a beautiful woman and her old, injured maid."

"And where are they now?" the large man asked.

"The old woman has gone to see the doctor. And Judith," he paused as he backed up, motioning for Judith to move forward, "is here, my lord."

Judith cautiously stepped forward, but in the dim light, the two men could see nothing more than a faint outline.

"Toland, let the light in," the bigger man commanded.

Toland ran to the east side of the tent, untied the taut vellum wall, and pulled it back. With one swift motion, the room flooded with so much sunlight that Toland, Acwel, and Judith were forced to shield their eyes, but the large man in the center of the room barely squinted. Judith stood still as her eyes adjusted to the light.

"Judith," the large man spoke.

When she heard her name, Judith finally looked up. Her imagination had led her to think Holofernes would look like a barbaric monster with fire in his eyes and sharp fangs protruding from his mouth, and her first impressions in the darkness had confirmed her deepest fears. As the lord moved closer, she half expected to see horns and a tail.

However, once he was close enough to be properly studied, Judith found herself relaxing a bit in his presence. His girth was not quite what she first assumed. He was adorned in beautiful, thick animal furs. Even with the heavy garments, his defined musculature was clearly visible.

As her eyes adjusted further, she could see that his unique look was not altogether unpleasant, nor was it frightening. He did not have a beard; she was mistaken about that. He was practically clean-shaven, but the bit of morning scruff that covered the bottom half of his face had looked fuller from a distance. His nose was stately, as refined as a Roman's, and his brows were thick, though not unruly. *His olive skin is beautiful*, Judith thought. She had never seen anything like it. Though he had a long scar on the left side of his face that stretched from his mouth to his temple, there was something distinguished and delightfully mysterious about it.

And his eyes. Judith found herself getting lost in their deep brown pools. *His eyes look so kind.* Indeed, everything about the man looked kind, and he had a sort of charisma that drew her in and made her feel welcome.

"My dear lady," he said with a deep and velvety voice. "Welcome to our camp. I am Lord Holofernes."

As Holofernes spoke, he gave a slight bow, and Judith felt obligated to give a low curtsy in return. Then with a small grin on his face and an amused light radiating from his eyes, he continued.

"Tell me, my dear, how did you stumble upon our camp?"

Judith took a moment to collect herself. She knew she needed to choose her words carefully. This was the pivotal moment that would decide her fate. This man could either take her in or execute her right here and now.

Before she spoke, she bowed low to the ground again, and then raising herself back up, she hid her fear, looked directly into Holofernes's eyes.

"My great lord, I am nothing but a poor peasant woman who escaped the horrors of my lord. He violated women, harmed children, and left his thanes starving. If anyone refused to bend to his will, he would kill them. So, when some days ago he demanded I become his wife, I escaped.

"When everyone in the village was fast asleep, Nerienda, my handmaid, and I made our escape. We ran all night without rest, following a river away from our home. In the morning we took cover, and though we could hear our lord and his dogs, horses, and men searching for us, we were too well hidden to be discovered. For four more nights we continued on without food, resting only during the day, until we were sure we were far from home. We had plans to continue on to the nearest town when my dear companion fell and twisted her ankle, and we could go no further. Not knowing what else to do, we prayed for a savior, and our prayers were answered when we were discovered by your guard, Acwel, this morning.

"I humbly ask you to allow us to stay with you for a little while, before sending us out on our own again into the dark and dangerous woods. I know I am now an outcast. I have chosen this for my servant and myself. But, believe me, my lord, when I say that being an outcast is a far better fate than being my lord's wife."

Judith completed her tale with another bow. Then she stood trembling, not knowing what Holofernes would do.

The mighty man looked down at the pale and frightened woman. Her story seemed honest, but how could he be sure she was not a spy?

"How does a peasant woman come to have such beautiful jewelry and clothes? I have known many peasant women, but none dressed so nobly as you."

Judith bowed her head. "My lord, the night the lord of my village came to me with a marriage proposal, I said yes for I feared death if I refused him. He wanted to show everyone how well he treated me, so he gave me these silver slippers and dress and gifted me with the most beautiful jewelry in the village…all in preparation for the wedding and feast taking place the following day. While everyone in town was asleep, I donned the outfit and jewelry, the only things of value that I owned, and left hastily. I knew I might need the jewelry to buy us a place in a community willing to take us in."

Judith paused and immediately took an inventory of herself to see if there was anything she was wearing that resembled a peasant's dress. Then her hand flew to her throat where her necklace was.

"The only thing I carry with me that is truly my own is this wooden bird on a strand of twine. My father carved it for me when I was a young girl, and I have never taken it off."

Holofernes nodded as he listened, and though he had an unsettling feeling about the story, he was also struck by Judith's beauty. He quickly ignored the voice of caution that whispered in the back of his mind. As Judith raised her eyes to meet his, he found himself lost in their sapphire brilliance.

"Alright, you may stay here for the day, and tonight you shall dine with me. Then I will decide if you will be permitted to remain with us longer. Acwel, see to it that Judith and her maid have a tent of their own to rest in. Give them everything they may need: food, water, comfortable bedding. Place guards at the tent's entrance, and bring Judith to dine with me this evening."

Judith smiled warmly; it was her first genuine smile of the morning. A feeling of relief washed over her as she recognized she had at least a chance for success.

"Thank you, my lord," she responded. "Acwel told me of your benevolence, but never in all my years could I have imagined a lord to be as kind and generous as you."

Holofernes laughed softly. "You are not only beautiful but wise as well. I will see you tonight." Then Holofernes turned back to his desk and instructed Toland to join him at the map.

Acwel led Judith from the tent and out into the open camp. "Follow me," he said. As they made their way along the winding path, the two moved in silence. Both were lost in thought as they contemplated their encounter with Holofernes. Acwel wondered if there would be a reward waiting for him at the upcoming feast, and Judith mused on the larger-than-life lord she was tasked with murdering.

"This tent is for you, my lady. The old woman is already inside, resting comfortably. I will have food brought to you at once," Acwel said. He pulled back the opening and with words of gratitude for his kindness, Judith entered the quiet haven.

CHAPTER 9

Judith was quickly bathed in a feeling of relief. Nerienda lay at the back of the tent in the dim candlelight. The old woman was resting comfortably, her right ankle propped up on a pile of furs. Judith ran to Nerienda and threw her arms around her neck. Nerienda held her tightly for a moment, happy to see the girl was all right. When she finally let go, she pulled back and looked into Judith's eyes.

"Tell me everything," the old woman said.

Judith began her story from the time the two women had separated. She spoke of the things she saw as she walked through the camp, including the men she encountered.

"Nerienda, these men are true warriors. They are far from home and are thirsty for battle. We must be careful of everything we say and do. We do not yet have Holofernes's protection and blessing, and the slightest misstep could compromise our task."

Nerienda nodded. "I saw things very much the same way. Aart was kind and carried me gently to the doctor. As we walked, he spoke of having a mother who looked just like me. This, I think, is what sparked his kindness. But the men we passed as we walked through the crowded camp were not so nice. They sneered, called names, and made unholy threats. Still, Aart kept them away and made sure I arrived safely to the doctor's tent."

Judith waited for Nerienda to continue her story, but instead the old woman asked, "Did you meet Holofernes? What did he look like? What did he say?"

"Acwel took me to the largest tent in the center of the camp, and there, in the middle of the dark room, Holofernes and his advisor were hunched over a large map, talking in the candlelight. When they saw us, they stopped what they were doing. After listening to my story, he told me we could stay here for the day. Tonight, I will join him for dinner, and then he will decide if we can remain in the camp as his guests."

Nerienda's eyes grew wide. "Judith, we must get you ready. There is so much to do." She made a move to stand, but Judith pushed her back down.

"No, Nerienda. Don't get up. You are supposed to be hurt, and should a guard enter and see you standing, we would be ruined."

Nerienda lay back down on the makeshift bed. "I'll stay in bed, but we need to fix your hair and touch up your make-up."

Judith nodded in agreement.

"Ask the guards outside for a few more candles and a bowl of water," Nerienda said.

The two women waited in silence for the items they requested. Once they had what they needed, Judith lit the candles. The single flame from earlier was not enough to see clearly, but four candles placed strategically around the small room gave a warm and friendly light.

Judith looked more closely at the tent surrounding her. It must have been assembled quickly: the few stitches holding it together were wide and hastily made. The hides were of different animals, some with the fur still on them, others not, and they seemed to simply lie over one another in certain areas with nothing but the weight of the layers keeping them from sliding off the tent's thin frame.

"Judith," Nerienda called softly, and Judith's concentration was broken. "We need to decide on our story."

Judith nodded as she adjusted her skirts and knelt down beside Nerienda's bed. As she did, Nerienda saw a flash of light near Judith's belt.

"Gracious, Judith. You aren't still wearing the dagger the blacksmith gave you? Take it off immediately and bury it in the food bag, what if someone were to find you with it. It would immediately give us away."

Judith turned pale as she realized her carelessness. She was about to utter something when Nerienda stopped her. "No matter. We both forgot it was there, but take it off now. It will stay hidden in the tent as long as we are here."

Judith did as she was told and then sat near Nerienda, close enough to whisper. The two women began to discuss the stories they had already shared with the guards and Holofernes, making sure to memorize all the details. To make things easier, they used as much of Judith's real life as they could.

The women carried on their whispered conversation for the better part of the day. While Judith talked, Nerienda braided her hair again, this time making the braiding more intricate. Judith found a few small boxes of black powder, rosy cream, and ruby paste at the bottom of their bag of belongings. She gave these to Nerienda, who smudged her cheeks with the rosy rouge and dabbed her lips with the ruby paste.

After Nerienda touched up Judith's make-up, she gave Judith

instructions for dinner. "Do not speak unless a question is asked of you. Do not eat before the lord has begun. You want him to be your lord, so be gracious. The only two things that can save us from death now are your charm and God's grace. Finally, whatever happens, do not remove your veil. Do not give him any reason to believe you are anything less than a noble maiden," Nerienda continued as she double-checked Judith's braid and fastened the girl's veil. "We seem to have time to carry out our plans. The army looks content for the moment. But while you are about in the camp, listen very carefully. If there is any indication the army may attack Bethulia, we must act quickly. Until then, be patient, watch, and listen."

At dusk, one of the guards entered the tent carrying a small loaf of bread and a meager portion of meat. He also carried a cup of mead and placed the meal next to Nerienda. Then he motioned for Judith to follow him.

Judith took a deep breath then stepped out of the tent. As she did so, she nearly ran into Knut.

"Where's Acwel?" she asked.

"The guard who had been placed on watch at her tent cleared his throat. "He is on guard duty at the far side of the camp. He keeps watch there at night, so Toland sent Knut to escort you to dinner."

Judith nervously looked up at the man who was nearly twice her size, but once again, he said nothing; he only grabbed her wrist as he set off at a brisk pace. Judith had to run to keep up, but she did her best to watch and listen. Unfortunately, all she could hear were jeers and lewd comments from the soldiers.

"Beautiful girl…have you ever had a cock in you? I can help you if you need someone to take care of that!"

"Don't listen to that dog, he can barely get his pecker up. I'm the one you want to see if you need some meat in your bones."

Judith shuddered as she was pulled through the camp. She looked up at Knut to see if he might put a stop to the harassment, but he didn't even seem to notice. Judith looked toward the sky and prayed. *Dear Lord, give me the strength and grace I need to get through this.*

The sky was several shades of blue, purple, orange, and pink, and the billowy clouds all seemed to shimmer in the light of the setting sun. The beauty and peace of the heavens calmed her, and Judith had nearly forgotten where she was when she ran into her escort. Knut's strong back was hard as a rock and running into him was painful. Judith had to make sure that her dress and veil were still in place. Once she was convinced nothing had been disturbed, she smoothed out her dress once more for good measure and took a moment to find her bearings. It was only then that she realized where they were.

She was standing outside the same large tent she had found herself in earlier that day. This time, however, there were two very different guards standing watch at the entrance. Both were shorter and stouter than Knut. Judith noticed they bore a striking resemblance to each other. *Brothers, perhaps*, she thought, though in the evening shadows she couldn't be certain.

While Knut spoke softly with the older of the two men, Judith began studying her surroundings just as Nerienda had instructed. The most noticeable quality was the near silence. The banter of the army sounded muffled and distant at the heart of the camp. Clearly the soldiers were stationed at the perimeter to keep watch and protect their lord.

She and the three guards were practically alone except for a group of men who sat around a nearby fire. They varied in age from quite young to old. The small group spoke in hushed whispers, though a laugh would occasionally escape from the circle and punctuate the silence. One of the men turned and caught her eye. His face was mapped with wrinkles, and his hair and beard were the color of silver, but his pale-blue eyes looked young and kind. He gave a small nod before turning back to his companions.

Suddenly, Judith heard a piercing cry above her and saw an eagle soaring through the shimmering clouds. She sucked in a sharp breath. Beasts of war seemed to be following her. First, the wolf in the woods, and now an eagle. She prayed no raven was near. Seeing all three animals in one day would most certainly mean war was imminent, and she did not want to be on the wrong side of the city walls when a battle broke out.

Knut and the older guard continued their conversation, discussing mundane war information, then their talk turned to the upcoming feast. Judith's ears perked up. *The men are planning on having a feast? When?*

She listened carefully, trying to remember everything so she could share it with Nerienda. It wasn't until the younger guard loudly cleared his throat and all three men turned toward her that Judith realized she had been so obviously eavesdropping. Knut eyed her suspiciously, but no one said a word. After several awkward minutes, Toland finally appeared at the doorway of the tent. Pulling the animal skins aside, he motioned for Judith and Knut to enter.

Even though it was the same tent Judith had entered early that morning, the inside was almost unrecognizable. The area was lit by dozens of candles, and the small table covered in maps had been replaced by a much larger, more ornate one with two silver place settings on top of it. Toland held out a chair for Judith, but she remained standing. It was considered rude to sit before a lord did, and she would not have her reputation marked by something so trivial.

Toland excused Knut and requested he wait outside. Before he left, the large man whispered something in Toland's ear. Judith saw him out of the corner of her eye, and cold sweat ran down the back of her neck. She knew he suspected her of something sinister, and though she could feel her knees about to buckle as Knut walked past on his way out the door, she did her best to raise herself to her fullest height and smile sweetly.

Judith was not kept waiting for long before Holofernes made a grand entrance. She realized he was even taller than she first thought. Much taller even than Knut. She gave a low bow to the lord.

"Please sit, my dear," he said as he walked over, took Judith's hand in his, and made a grand bow. Despite the theatrics, Judith felt his welcome was sincere.

Holofernes returned to his side of the table and heaved his large frame into the oversized, ornately decorated chair waiting for him. Judith continued standing until he was situated, and then she quickly settled into her own seat. Food was brought out and served, first to Holofernes and then to Judith. There was lamb stew with cabbage and potatoes, brown bread, roasted venison, and dried figs. It smelled divine. No one in Bethulia had seen such a lavish spread in months, and the mere sight of its decadence made Judith swoon.

Once their plates were full, with double portions given to Holofernes, the cook departed. Only Judith and Holofernes remained with Toland standing in the shadows. The room was silent.

Holofernes poured himself a cup of wine and filled Judith's glass as well. He took a long, slow drink as he studied the woman across from him. She was positively radiant in the glow of the candlelight.

What Holofernes could not see, though, was how terrified Judith was. Her legs shook and her heart raced as she sat across from the most intimidating man she had ever met. She didn't dare take a drink for fear the lord might see her hands tremble as she held her glass. She could feel how closely he was watching her, though she kept her eyes down. Finally, Holofernes broke the silence.

"Please eat, my lady. I'm sure the provisions you received for breakfast were no more than satisfactory, but tonight you and I shall eat well. Drink. This wine was seized from one of our recent conquests. The town was not far from here, and they were skilled at making a good drink. It is the most delicious I've had since being away from home."

Judith could hear her blood pumping in her ears. The sound was so loud that she barely heard Holofernes. Her breathing became labored, and she nearly jumped up and ran out of the tent back to Bethulia, but it was the memory of the last, far more meager supper she'd had that stopped her. For a split second, she was back home eating dinner with Cyneric, and she could hear his words from his first visit. *I trust no one else. If you do not accept this task, I fear all will be lost.*

Judith breathed deeply. Her pulse calmed and her mind cleared. Her courage and resolve returned, and her hands steadied. She looked up at Holofernes, smiled sweetly, and took a drink, struggling not to think about the hundreds of lives that had been lost to get the wine. "Delicious," she said.

Holofernes spent a few moments greedily devouring the food on his plate before he continued with a mouth full of lamb.

"We did not get a chance to speak much this morning. Please tell me where your home is."

"Home? Well, home is very far away, and it's been many years since I've seen her."

Toland stepped forward and refilled Holofernes's plate.

"Toland, how long has it been since we've seen home?"

Toland responded softly, "Three years, two months, and six days, my lord."

"Three years, two months, and six days," Holofernes repeated. "Hmm, that does sound about right. But we've been doing quite well for ourselves, haven't we?"

"Indeed, my lord."

"Indeed," Holofernes echoed. "But tell us, Judith, where do you come from that you have not heard of our great conquests?"

Judith smiled again, a smile she was quickly perfecting, and gathered her thoughts. She remembered all that she and Nerienda had discussed. Then taking one more sip of wine, she began.

"I'm originally from Brenton, my lord." Judith's eyes shone innocently.

"Brenton? I've never heard of it. Toland, where is this place?"

Toland stopped mid-serve and held a ladle of stew over Judith's bowl. "I don't know, my lord. I've never heard of it either."

Both men eyed Judith suspiciously, but she continued unbothered.

"It is a small town that lies to the east, just on the edge of the sea. It's very close to Ceolwich, the well-known seaside village famous for trading, which I'm sure you've heard of. All the finest merchants from the mysterious far eastern lands travel over the sea to bring their wares to the port. The small village where I grew up was only a short distance from it."

When Judith and Nerienda chose their town of origin, they decided upon a village that Judith knew much about. Brenton truly was a small fishing village, and the port city was the town her father always traveled to before departing for the east. This was a city whose great lord was more interested in trade and taxes than war. It was a two-day journey from Bethulia, but Judith and Nerienda were sure that Holofernes and his men from the north knew little about that area.

"And what does this land by the sea look like?" Toland sneered.

Holofernes held up a hand to silence him and then said ever so softly, "Tell us."

Judith had gone to the port city with her father only once. It was the one time she had left Bethulia, and though she had only been seven, she remembered the trip as if it had happened yesterday.

"The first thing you notice," she began with a smile as she reminisced, "is the smell of the sea. Even before you can see the smoke rising from the chimneys, the smell of salt and brine greets you in a great rush." Judith couldn't help but feel swept up in the memory.

"The harbor is not large, just big enough for a few boats, and they are nearly always out during the day. As you come around the bend to enter the little town, you stand on a high hill. From it, you can see for miles out to sea. The trading ships, with their bright billowed sails of red, green, and black glide effortlessly over the water heading to the port just a few miles north.

"My father worked for a merchant trader. He would buy the bright bolts of cloth and fabric that were brought over to the port city and sell them to men who traveled near and far to pay for the rare fabrics. Most who came to his shop were stewards of great men wanting the most beautiful fabrics for their lords and ladies."

Holofernes smiled but did not say anything. Toland, however, had questions. "If you lived in such an elegant fashion, why did you say you were a peasant girl?"

Judith's eyes grew wide. "I didn't live elegantly. My father would leave before dawn and walk the few miles to work every morning and return after dark every night. Our home was small and, though we had enough to get by, we never had more than we needed. When I was still a child, my father passed away. Because I had no mother, a lady of a wealthy nearby town took me in and raised me as her own. Her husband, the lord, often did business with my father and was one of the first to learn of his passing. Though I was not nobility by birth, she saw to it that I was treated like part of her family. I learned to sing, sew, and play the harp as well as any noble child.

"However, only a few years later, our town was overtaken by a lord from the south. He had spent an entire winter preparing to occupy our city. At first thaw, his men came and burned our town. They took our gold and killed our lord. Thinking that I was nobility, the thanes brought me to their lord, and he took me back home to Atwood with him. I lived in Atwood for seven years as a captive, living the life of a peasant. The only comfort afforded to me was the maid assigned to assist me."

"And why was the marriage happening only now? Why did your lord wait for seven years?" Holofernes asked with narrowed eyes.

Judith bowed her head in feigned embarrassment, then timidly said, "He was already married, my lord. The queen was ill, but she was loved by everyone. No one would have ever heard of him dismissing her on account of her illness. Had he done so, there surely would have been an uprising. He cares far more about his power than about anything else, so he waited until her death to marry me. It was barely four days after her passing that he announced I was to be his new queen and ordered the wedding feast to be prepared."

"And how long did you say you have been running from those chasing you?"

Judith's face grew solemn.

"We began the day before the wedding was to occur. Well after midnight, when everyone was asleep, we ran as fast as we could. But we stopped to hide at first light. The search party passed by in the late afternoon but did not find us. When dusk settled, we ran again. We did this five nights in a row, praying that we would not run into any danger. Then, just when my dear maid felt she could go on no further with her twisted ankle, we collapsed in a thicket of brush and prayed someone would find us.

"We have been treated well here. My maid is feeling better, and she now has a comfortable bed, at least for one night. I cannot thank you enough."

Holofernes was beaming at the accolades Judith was showering on him. The arrival of a woman with nothing more than her handmaid was extremely unusual, but Judith's beauty was mesmerizing. As Holofernes sat there watching the maiden enjoy her dinner, Toland leaned down to whisper something in his ear. Judith noticed his movements and knew he was most likely about to pass on the message Knut had given him. Before Toland could say anything to his lord, Judith spoke up.

"If I may be so bold, my lord. I heard the guards speaking of an upcoming feast. I love feasts and have not been to one in ages. I would never permit myself to attend the feast of strangers, but perhaps you could tell me when it will take place?"

Holofernes gave a wide, charming grin. "My dear lady, our feasts could not be grander. We have the best scop, mead, and stories in all the land. My men fight well, and they are rewarded for their honorable efforts. I bestow gifts of gold, treasure, and rings that other lords could only hope to have in their possession. Tomorrow we must tour the camp, so I can introduce you to my best soldiers and show you the treasures we have won."

Tomorrow. He said tomorrow, Judith thought to herself. She gave a warm smile and a small nod. "I would be honored, my lord."

Toland leaned forward again to speak, but Holofernes dismissed him with a wave. "Very well. It is settled. Tomorrow you shall see the great work I have done."

Holofernes was nearly finished eating by this time, but he found himself lingering over his last few bites, not wishing his dinner guest to leave. He continued to ask questions of her home where she grew up, and in turn Judith painted a relatively truthful picture of her life as a child.

She shared her favorite stories from her father and found herself lowering her guard as she spoke. The night wore on, but she and Holofernes were so lost in conversation they hardly realized time passed at all. It turned out the two had far more in common than they ever thought possible, and they spoke of all their favorite childhood stories that made each other laugh.

Judith couldn't help but begin to feel a certain amount of affection for the man in front of her, and the feeling appeared to be mutual. During one brief lull in the conversation, Holofernes's eyes met hers, and she found herself getting lost in their dark pools. He seemed to be able to look past her physical beauty and see directly into her soul. She felt a flame flicker deep within her heart, and the warmth traveled down to her toes. She gave a beautiful smile in return that caused Holofernes to laugh out loud before returning to their conversation.

As they carried on, it felt as if they had known each other all their lives. It was only after they heard Toland's snores from the far corner of the tent that they finally wrapped up their conversation with promises to continue it the next day.

Holofernes called Toland over to the table, and the man jumped to attention while attempting to rub the sleep from his eyes.

"Toland, see to it that Judith returns to her tent safely. Have two men stand on guard tonight so that no one disturbs her or her maid."

"As you wish, sir," he replied with a bow.

Grabbing Judith by the wrist, Toland quickly escorted her back to her tent. Just before she was about to say good night, the thane leaned in and in the faintest whisper said, "I don't know who you are or why you are here. But I do not trust you. Remember, you are only one weak woman in a sea of a thousand men. Don't do anything foolish."

Toland's words caught Judith off guard, and she was thankful that darkness had settled long ago. She was sure Toland could not see the worry on her face, but for good measure she kept her head bowed.

"I do not want any trouble, only a place to stay for the night. Please thank your lord for his kindness to us. Good night, Toland," she said.

The thane's eyes narrowed, and he let her wrist drop from his grasp as he barked out orders to the two men guarding the tent's entrance.

"Guard them both. Make sure neither leaves this tent until Knut comes to get the maiden in the morning. The old woman stays where she is."

The guards nodded in unison as Judith crept inside, filled with terror from the threat she had just received.

CHAPTER 10

It was nearly morning, but Judith was still wide awake inside their dark tent. Nerienda was sleeping peacefully next to her, but Judith was trembling with fear. Things were not going according to plan. However, her dinner with Holofernes held many pleasant surprises. Every time she closed her eyes, she saw Holofernes's dark features, and his piercing eyes stared straight through her once again. This sort of stare would normally have invoked anxiety in her, but with Holofernes, it only sparked a fire deep inside her… a small one, but one of desire.

The rumors had made the army and their lord out to be savage monsters. *But these men… they are just men,* Judith thought. *Disgusting, yes, but far from animals. Maybe Cyneric was wrong. Maybe Holofernes isn't the man who pillaged and raped thousands upon thousands. Maybe this isn't the man who murdered hundreds in their beds while they slept. Maybe this man, the one I'm meant to kill, is not so bad after all. Perhaps his intentions are good, and the horror stories of the wars and battles are only hearsay told by the scops to scare their audience. I was sent to kill a monster. How can I kill a man?*

Judith tossed and turned for the rest of the night, drifting in and out of sleep. Holofernes filled her thoughts and dreams alike. She could not think of a single man in Bethulia who was as exotic and handsome as him.

Judith was nervous that she might be found out. Toland and Knut certainly felt that she was a danger to them; she needed to stay on her guard. As she lay in bed, she realized that she still had the small blade from the blacksmith in the food bag. *It could be what saves us,* she thought to herself.

As fears and worries filled her head, there was one part of her that was hopeful to spend more time with Holofernes the coming day. Perhaps she had been sent here not to murder the warlord but to win him over in some way. Perhaps she could get him to turn around and go home. Perhaps she could even get him to take her with him. She didn't have much she was leaving behind. Maybe instead of Judith being the salvation for her city, Holofernes was *her* salvation. With a soft smile on her delicate lips, Judith gave a deep sigh and finally fell asleep.

***

Two hours later she was awakened by the sound of the bustling camp. There were animals bleating, hammers pounding, and shouts of directions flying through the air. Slightly confused as to where she was and what was going on, Judith sat up and scanned her surroundings. It wasn't until her eyes adjusted that she remembered she was in Holofernes's camp in a tent far from her home, preparing to kill the leader of the army that guarded her.

Holofernes… She let the rest of the thought linger, not daring to finish it.

Moments later, a guard entered the tent with a small loaf of bread, a few clumps of cheese, and a large cup of mead. Soon, he returned with a small bowl of water for the two women to wash their hands and face. Judith quickly cleaned herself up, then went over to Nerienda and gently shook her shoulder. The old woman's eyes snapped open. It seemed to take her a moment to remember where she was and all the goings on of the day before. But then the startled look quickly faded from her face.

"What happened last night? What decision did Holofernes make? Are we to stay with him?" she asked.

Judith smiled when she thought of Holofernes. "We had a lovely evening, with some of the best food I have ever eaten. Certainly the best since the siege started."

Judith then went on to explain the details of the dinner and to discuss everything they had talked about. She was happy to be thinking again about the dark, handsome man from dinner. She was hoping that soon Nerienda would see the Holofernes she was beginning to know.

"Perhaps," she mused more to herself than her companion, "Holofernes is not the monster we all thought he was."

Nerienda looked at Judith with a penetrating stare. She wasn't sure what her young charge meant, but she was certain she did not like the words coming from her mouth.

As soon as the phrase escaped her lips, Judith realized she had gone too far. Nerienda's cold stare told her that what she had suggested was beyond reproach and must never be thought of or brought up again.

After a long moment, Nerienda let out a sigh. "Tell me. What are today's plans?"

"I will take a tour of the camp with Holofernes today. He would like to take me around and show me all the treasures his men have amassed during their time away from home."

Judith chose her words carefully so as not to show how eager she was to spend more time with the lord. She explained that Holofernes would decide what to do with them after the tour. Judith was quite sure they were safe with him—far safer than they would be in Bethulia, where an attack was imminent.

Nerienda and Judith began their breakfast, eating in silence. Once finished, Judith did what she could to make herself presentable for her meeting. Soon, the guard entered the tent and beckoned Judith to follow him. He seemed friendly, and his smaller stature made him more approachable. He whistled happily as he led Judith through the camp. They did not go to the large tent that Knut and Acwel had taken her to. Instead, they veered to the right and stopped outside a slightly smaller one just off to the side of the main area. Then the man instructed Judith to stay where she was and wait for him.

When he entered the tent, Judith caught a glimpse of the elaborate and expensive-looking room inside. *This must be Holofernes's private quarters,* she thought. She didn't see much, just a bed with some sort of canopy over it. Flashes of gold, bright blue, green and red... all beautiful and vibrant. She wondered at the beauty hidden within.

Judith waited patiently and looked up at the sky, scanning for ravens, but she didn't see any. *I've fought a wolf. We've seen an eagle. But no ravens yet, even though they usually arrive with the other two. Perhaps we were all wrong about the plan. Maybe there won't even be a battle. Perhaps, this time, Bethulia will be spared, and I will be able to escape.*

CHAPTER 11

Holofernes exited the tent as gregarious as always. Judith let out a small gasp when she saw him standing right next to her. This was the closest he had been to her, and she had not realized he was so much taller than her. She barely passed his elbow. His broad muscles made him appear stronger than any man she'd ever met. Once again, though, it was his dark-brown eyes staring into hers that made the flicker of the candlelight deep within her burn more intensely. Judith gave a slight nod and a low curtsy.

"Good morning, my lord. I hope you slept well last night. It is a pleasure and privilege to spend time with you this morning."

Holofernes liked her greeting. It was one he hoped all his subjects would give him eventually, though at the moment not everyone was willing to commit to it. The radiant woman before him was breathtaking. He had never seen such beauty in all his travels. He gave a warm smile and held out his arm for her.

"Come, my lady, let me show you around. I'm sure you will be impressed with everything my thanes have done. Come. The day is only beginning, but we have much to see."

Judith looked up into Holofernes's face, and though his features were dark, there appeared to be a softness about him that she found comforting. Neither Knut nor Toland had such a softness to them. Holofernes was different. Something about the way he carried himself showed him to be more like nobility than warrior. He had a regal air that resonated with Judith.

Holofernes smiled at her and gently patted her hand, which was now resting on the crook of his arm, and began leading her through the camp.

"As you know, our feast begins in two days' time, and all the men are getting ready for it. It has been months since any of them had a decent meal, and it's been even longer since I bestowed gifts upon my best warriors. Tomorrow night will be a joyous celebration before we go into battle against the Bethulians. Have you ever heard of Bethulia?"

Judith smiled and innocently shook her head. "My lord," she said, "I come from the east and have no knowledge of the towns around here. Had we known there was a town, we certainly would have run to it, but now I am happy to have run into your camp instead."

Holofernes gave a small laugh as they made their way around the winding maze of tents. They began toward the center and worked their way to the outer edges stopping frequently to watch the many preparations. They spent several minutes inspecting a long table several men were waxing for the feast. They wandered through the livestock pens and admired the plump goats, sheep, and steers.

As they continued on their way, the bright sun shone overhead. It was a clear day; the air was crisp and cool. There was not a single cloud in the sky, and once again, Judith looked around for any sign of ravens. Still, none were to be seen. Stepping lightly around the tents, she listened as Holofernes told her about the men they were passing.

"There is Magen." He called out to him with a wide wave. "He took on ten men in battle at once—and killed them all. And there is Seaver." He called out again. "He once killed a lord with his bare hands." Holofernes laughed at the memory. "Seaver has a crooked nose, but don't ever point it out. The lord he killed found that out the hard way!"

The tour continued, and Holofernes took Judith around to each of his officers for introductions. Each man was called upon by rank and name, and he introduced her as the queen of Atwood. Judith certainly looked the part. Her dress could have belonged to any queen in the land. She conducted herself in a way that made it easy to assume she was of noble birth. She spoke genteelly and had a gracefulness about her that was attractive, especially to the soldiers, who had not spoken to a woman in many months. They had certainly assaulted their share of women, but to have a conversation with one who was introduced as a queen was something few had ever done.

It took all morning for Judith to meet everyone. At noon, they began to make their way back to the center of camp for lunch in the familiar great tent. The whole day, thus far, had proved to be delightful, and the man before her seemed far from the monster Cyneric painted him to be. Halfway back to the tent, though, they rounded a corner, and four goats that had escaped their pen ran in front of them, knocking Judith to the ground. Stunned for a moment, Judith took her time picking herself up.

Seeing Judith fall, Holofernes flew into a rage, grabbed the nearest of the goats and snapped its neck as he roared after the others. "Get out of here, you three, before I kill you too." Then, turning to the nearest thane, he shouted, "Go get them, you daft fool, before I wring your neck too." The young man took off after the goats before Holofernes could say anything else.

Breathing heavily, the lord turned to Judith. When he saw that she was upright, he gave a slight cough, collected himself, and carried on as if nothing had happened.

"Did you happen to see the fine workmanship on the central tent? Be sure to look closely at how seamlessly my men have pieced the animal skins together," he said.

"I will be sure to take note of it," Judith responded as she stared at the dead goat, shocked not only at what she was looking at but also confused that the altercation ended so abruptly. She struggled to find anything else to say, and the two walked the rest of the way in uneasy silence.

Once they arrived at the tent, Judith noticed they were not the only two present today. The tent was being prepared for the feast. The animal skin walls were pulled back so the air could pass through freely. Extra space was being prepared to allow for the entire camp to fit comfortably under the canopy of animal skins.

Judith did notice the craftmanship. However, she kept quiet about the fact that the extensions, while impressive, were not quite as well prepared as the original tent. She suspected that these outer areas would be reserved for the lower-ranking soldiers. She noticed a few cushions being set up in a corner, and large fire pits were built around the outer perimeter of the tent to give light to the feast. Though Judith knew little about the finer details of feasts between thanes and lords, she knew the celebration would last long into the night, and possibly into the morning.

Holofernes invited her to sit down to eat. The meal was simpler than it had been the night before. There was cold lamb, a few boiled potatoes, and a plate of cold vegetables to share. Holofernes was given a large loaf of bread, and he broke off a small piece of crust for Judith. The rest he used to sop up the juice from the lamb. He ate hungrily while Judith politely nibbled at her food.

Holofernes seemed fully immersed in his meal. Not only had he stopped talking to Judith, but he also completely stopped looking at her. Judith remembered how important it was to engage him, and she knew the best way to get him to speak was by asking him to talk about himself.

"Tell me," she said, "where do you and your men come from?"

Holofernes put down his food, threw back his head, and laughed. "Have you not heard, my dear?"

"I've heard whispers from your men that you come from the far north," she said, "but that is all."

Holofernes smiled, brushed his hands off, wiped his mouth with his sleeve, and began.

"The town my men and I departed from is in the far north. However, I was not originally from there. I was born in the deep forest of the Celts. My mother was a Celtic witch, and my father died before I was born. My mother was an outcast, witches often are, especially ones with children and no husband. As a child, I had no friends and no one to care for me except my mother, who was often too sick to look after me. She was a weak woman both in body and spirit. She could never stand up for herself when others looked down on her, but her one conviction was in her potions and spells. They never did us any good, but she refused to abandon them. She was a bit crazy perhaps," he mused, forgetting for a moment that Judith was there. He shook his head, trying to shake the shame of the memories.

"The men in my village lived in fear of the Angles and Saxons. They would try all sorts of ancient incantations and prayers to keep them away—pagan sorcery, your people call it—which rarely worked. Instead, we were always driven deeper and deeper into the thick woods and high hills. But I was not born to run. I was born to fight. Not long after my fourteenth birthday, I decided to travel to the Anglo-Saxon land and stake my claim as their leader. The men in my village refused to believe that I would ever succeed. They told me I would be dead in a matter of days, but I didn't listen. I promised myself that I would kill the leader of the first town I came to and make myself lord."

Judith looked at him in amazement. "You must have been very brave. How did you train for such a battle?" she asked.

Holofernes smiled. "There was one man who looked on me kindly: an old blacksmith who had little work since we'd been driven into the forest. His uncle had been a great warrior and had taught him how to fight at a young age. Because I had no friends and he had no work, we often spent our days together. He taught me how to fight with a sword, smash a man's skull with a hammer, and crush a man's throat with my bare hands."

Judith looked at him in wonder and without thinking blurted out, "And had you ever killed a man before you left home?"

Holofernes looked at her with penetrating eyes. The flame in Judith's heart seemed to take root deeper and deeper in her belly.

"Yes, I had," he said, "just one on the night before I left. Up until then it had only been birds, rabbits, small game. Some for food, of course, and some for sport. The man I killed was a wanderer who stumbled upon our home after being cast out by the Anglo-Saxons. He was a large man with blond hair and blue eyes. I'd never seen anyone like him up close before. Late one night, he came to our hut. No one knew he was there because we lived on the outskirts of the village.

"When he entered our home, he started eating our food. Then seeing my mother, who was quite beautiful, he moved toward her with his dirty hands reaching out to grab her, muttering something

I couldn't understand at the time. Later I learned he was saying, 'You are mine now. This is my new home, and I am never leaving.'

"His foreign words sounded soft and sweet, but I knew we were in danger, so I had to do something. Before he knew it, my hands were around his neck. His eyes bulged out, and his face turned purple in the dim firelight. I crushed his throat, just as I'd been trained to do. He was the first man I'd ever killed. The moment I felt his life leave his body was exhilarating, a high I had to feel again. I knew in that moment that I was a warrior and not a coward who fled from danger."

Holofernes paused for a moment with a wild look in his eyes. Judith was taken aback by his story, but he spoke the last words so softly she was not entirely sure she'd heard him correctly.

"My lord, you acted with courage, and your mother must have been proud. But why wouldn't any men in your village fight but you?"

"They were always outnumbered at least two to one when any of the Angles or Saxons came to overtake our village. Besides, they didn't have the foresight to train. No one did except the smith and me."

Judith nodded in understanding. "Please continue. How did you come to be lord?"

"The morning after I killed our nighttime visitor, I dragged him into the village and laid him on the ground for everyone to see. I called out to the men and said, 'This man came into our home last night. He tried to attack my mother, but I stopped him. Now I am going to his village to destroy his lord. Is there anyone who wants to go with me?'

"The men—old, young, strong, weak—all just stared at me. Though many were bigger than me, all were cowards. Everyone just assumed the man was the first of many to come and attack us. Instead of fighting, they wanted to head farther west, farther away from the new peoples who were coming once again to displace us just as they had before.

"Before I even finished speaking, some had already started packing and calling out orders to move again, but I was done running. I went to my mother and told her of my departure. Instead of crying or wishing me to stay, she gave me some of her most potent herbs and magic crystals and told me to keep them close to my heart. I asked if she was moving with the others, but she said, 'No, I am done running. I will stay where I am, so you will always know where home is.'"

Holofernes paused in his story and gazed into the distance. "If I ever go back and cannot find her, it will be because she has passed on, not because she ran."

There was a brief moment of silence before he turned to look at Judith and continued.

"The Celtic people I grew up with were neither the strongest nor the bravest, but one thing they were good at was knowing how to navigate the land. I learned how to track and hunt before I could talk. I became an expert at maneuvering through the dense woods without getting lost—woods so thick with trees they blocked out the sun at high noon. These were things that were bred into all our people, and these are the advantages that make me the great warlord I am."

Judith sat in amazement, completely enraptured by all that Holofernes was telling her.

"It took me three days to reach the Angles," he continued. "Just like you, I walked, and I ran. But I never stopped. I ate what food I found along the way. The morning of the third day, I stumbled into the first Anglo town I came across. I knew the Angles were warriors who never backed down from a fight, and I knew that my best chance for gaining power and respect quickly was to fight their leader and win. As you know, the leader is supposed to be the strongest and wisest. If you can defeat him in battle, you can make the others loyal to you... and that is what I did. I demanded that their lord fight me in battle. He was a large man, practically the size of Knut, with even more muscle.

"He came up to me, just a boy at the time, asking what I wanted. I could not understand him and started to speak in my own language. It did not take long for an old woman to step in and act as a translator. Once I understood his question, I told him I wanted to be the lord of the peoples who had destroyed my home. He laughed at me and said that was an ambitious goal and that the very first step would not be to fight him but to fight one of his soldiers. I scoffed at this and said, 'I will fight you or no one.'

"He looked me up and down and replied, 'You are not worth my time. Fight the man I choose, and if you defeat him, I'll consider fighting you.'

"So, I grabbed a sword from the nearest soldier, and the king pointed to a thane to join me. The men laughed at my size. I was skinny, underfed, and tired. They never expected a boy from the woods to have the skill to defeat a thane in armed combat.

"We began our combat with swords, but I quickly disarmed him. Once that happened, I threw my sword aside and did what I did best—I fought with my hands. My first punch broke his nose, then I kicked him in the shin, bringing him to his knees. Eventually I found his neck, just as I had with the man who came to our tent. After the sound of his breaking neck echoed through the air and he fell to the ground, I looked at the king and asked, 'Will you fight me now?'

"He just smiled and called another man forward. The soldier marched toward me. He was bigger and stronger than the first, and he carried a hammer with him. Seeing this, I picked up a rock, and the two of us fought. I dodged him as best I could and eventually knocked him to the ground by tripping him. Once he was on the ground, I smashed his skull with my makeshift weapon. It took more than one blow, but in the end I won."

"Were you hurt?" Judith asked.

"Yes, the man broke a bone in my hand and one good punch to the face gave me a broken nose and two black eyes, but I wasn't about to let that stop me. I had come to the town with one goal in mind, and I was determined to reach it or die trying. Instead of complaining, I turned to the lord and with swollen, half-shut eyes I shouted, 'Now will you fight me?'

"Again, he called another name. I was growing impatient and wondering why he was doing all this, but then I realized that he didn't underestimate me. Never once had he thought I couldn't defeat him. This is a very important lesson to every lord—one must never underestimate what his opponent can do."

Judith began to tremble. Holofernes spoke while staring directly into her eyes, and she felt she had just been exposed. She feared he could see her for the fraud she was, but she did her best to conceal her emotions.

"What was the king's motive then, other than trying to have others kill you instead of him?" Judith asked to hide her nervousness.

Holofernes nodded and pointed a finger to her as if giving a lesson.

"The lord was trying to wear me down. He was trying to make me so tired that by the time it was his turn to fight me, I wouldn't have any strength left. And more importantly, he was studying me... understanding how I moved, how I fought, what my strategies and tactics were. He understood the importance of knowing these things. The third man he called had an axe with him and handed one to me as well. The thane felt sorry for me because I looked so hurt, and he gave me a shield even though he refused to use one. I took it because I knew he had the upper hand, and I did not want to be defeated before I had a chance to fight the lord. I had come too far to die now.

"Our battle lasted for the better part of the morning, but I didn't relent. I grew tired and weak, but we continued to fight. Finally, I got lucky—the soldier let his guard down, and for a brief moment he exposed his left flank to me. I swung hard with my axe and thrust it so deep into his side that it split his heart in two. He fell to his knees, and with blood spurting out of his mouth, he crashed to the ground.

"I looked at the lord and repeated my question for the third time that day, 'Now will you fight me?' He smiled and shook his head. 'You're a foolish boy,' he said. 'You should never have come here.' He called one last person forward, a boy this time. At first everyone laughed at the thought of me fighting one of the weakest men in the town, but the lord knew what he was doing."

Judith was sitting on the edge of her seat by this time. With every word Holofernes spoke, her eyes got a bit larger, and she leaned in closer to hear what he was saying. Holofernes noticed his captivated audience and was telling the story as well as any scop at any mead hall.

"The boy," he said, "couldn't have been more than my age, and he looked like me except for his blond hair and blue eyes. We were both tall and thin, scrawny and underfed. As he walked forward, the lord nodded to him and said something in a low voice that I couldn't hear. He carried nothing with him but a rusty sword.

"Everyone in the village was intrigued, and the circle around us grew even tighter. Finally, a horn blew, and the boy lunged toward me. He fought like no one I'd ever fought before. He moved the same way I did.

"You see," Holofernes continued, "the lord had been watching me while I fought his best thanes. He saw how I moved. He saw my technique. He understood after only three rounds of fighting that though I was smaller than the other men, I was quicker. I used my size to my advantage by slipping in and out of their heavy blows. However, my size was not an advantage against the boy. My moves and my quickness were now of no help because this boy was exactly like me.

"We fought for a long time, each of us gaining on the other a little and then losing ground. By the time the battle came to the last blow, the gray dusk of evening was settling in. Finally, at long last, the boy became too exhausted, and with one quick clash of swords he collapsed to the ground. I was about to finish him off when the lord stepped forward and grabbed my arm. He said something once again in his foreign tongue. 'The best lords act with mercy,' the old woman who was my translator shouted to me in the hopes that I would spare the boy's life.

"It turned out the young boy was the son of a farmer. He had little experience fighting other than fending off wild animals that tried to eat the crops, but he turned out to be a worthy opponent, and he fought more bravely than any of the other men that day. Certainly, he had more courage. It seems the less experience you have at something, the more courage you need to succeed. I released my grip on the boy, and he fell to the ground. Before anyone else could act, I walked over to where the boy had been standing with his father. The family dog was with him, and in one swift stroke of the blade, I sliced its throat. No one said a word."

"The poor dog. He was innocent," Judith whispered.

"I took one life to spare another. I had to show I could be merciful but also just," Holofernes explained matter-of-factly.

"What happened to the boy afterward?" Judith asked.

"It took him a full week to recover, but he became one of my dearest, closest friends and confidants," Holofernes replied with a look toward Toland.

Judith looked at him as well, and though Toland and Holofernes looked nothing alike, she could see the slight resemblance in stature that may have existed when they were younger. Toland smiled, but Judith noticed that it did not reach his eyes. They were sad. *He loved that dog*, she realized.

Then Toland gave a slight bow toward his lord and went back to shouting orders for the preparations for the feast.

"Please go on, sir. What happened between you and the lord?"

Holofernes smiled and gave a slight shake of his head as he thought back to the fateful day that had determined the course of the rest of his life.

"You see, while the lord had been studying me, I had been studying him too. Throughout the day, I noticed he never moved his left arm. It stayed akimbo at his side. He carried himself with great strength, but I realized that his left side must have been wounded in battle at one time or another. It was no longer of any real use to him.

"It was easy to grant mercy to the boy on the ground in front of me, but I knew if I wanted to become lord, I could not be weak-hearted. I could not show mercy to those who thought they were my superiors, especially on my first day.

"The lord bent over my last opponent. While he knelt on the

ground unarmed and completely unsuspecting of any attack, I grabbed him from behind, surprising him, and held my sword's blade up to his throat. I purposely held him on the left side where I knew he would be immobile, and with one swift motion, I sliced open his neck.

"As you know, Angles and Saxons are an honorable lot and fight with that same honor they uphold in the rest of their lives, but the Celtic people fight by any means necessary. This is the reason I always carry my sword with me. You never know just when the enemy could strike, and it's best to be ready. I even hang it over my bed at night so it is in easy reach should someone choose to attack me while I'm sleeping. I'm never without it, and that is why I have remained lord for so long."

He showed Judith the sword he carried at his side. It was beautiful, made of gold, silver, and very fine strong metal. It shimmered in the afternoon light.

She nodded in understanding. "Truly a wise thing," she said softly.

Holofernes laughed and said, "That is not wise. That is only practical." Then he continued. "If we want to win, we fight to secure our victory, and that is what I have trained my men to do as well. Isn't that right, Toland?"

Toland looked over at Holofernes and gave a small smile. "It is, my lord."

Holofernes seemed to be beaming with pride at all his men had accomplished, and he looked at Judith as he continued his story.

"The lord fell to the ground with blood pouring from his neck. He did not have long to live, and it was clear to everyone that I had taken control of their village. A feast was held in my honor as the new lord of the region that very night. The day after, I began training my men in the ways of the Celts. I taught them to track, hunt, and fight just as the blacksmith had taught me. It served me well in battle, so I knew it would serve us well as an army. This is why we have been so successful all across this land.

"When I exited that thick forest and entered the Anglo-Saxon world, I did not want to be lord of a village. The men and women from across the sea took my Celtic home, and I am determined to win it back. I intend to rule the entire land, and that is just what we are doing, isn't it, Toland?"

Toland nodded again. "It is, my lord."

His response was sure and steady, but Judith noticed a look of concern on his face. She smiled sweetly so as to appear completely innocent.

"Tell me, my lord, how exactly have you been able to defeat so many people?"

Holofernes laughed. "We weaken them before we attack, if necessary by cutting off their supplies of food and water, and we attack when they are asleep or surprise them at first light. Either way, we make sure that our enemies never see us coming."

Judith nodded.

Toland could no longer ignore the conversation. He interrupted, "My lord, if you are done with lunch, surely our guest would like to continue with the tour."

Holofernes looked at him for a moment and then nodded. He was no fool; he understood that even with someone as beautiful, fair, and innocent as the maiden sitting in front of him, giving away too many details of the army's strategies could be deadly. He stood up, walked over to Judith, and graciously escorted her out of the tent and back into the bright afternoon sun.

CHAPTER 12

Judith shuddered at the thought of Holofernes killing so many people in cold blood, but she dutifully walked behind him as they continued their tour of the camp. She found it difficult to believe the man standing before her could be anything but benevolent and fair. He didn't seem like a cold-blooded killer. Even the old sword he carried at his waist appeared rusty and out of use. *He has surely softened with age. After all, it is hard to always thirst for power and blood. I'd suppose one would grow tired of violence and long for the peaceful reassurances of friends and family.*

Judith met most of the men at Holofernes's camp before lunch, but there were still a few introductions left, including the group of men Judith had seen the night before around the campfire. They proved to be Holofernes's advisors, and the old man with blue eyes was called Beartwold. Too old to fight, he was the one who stayed behind at the camp and counseled the lord before and after each battle. Holofernes claimed he was the wisest man he'd ever known, and Judith believed him.

Once the introductions were complete, Holofernes took Judith to one of the camp's far corners. She immediately noticed that the area was more heavily guarded than the rest. Whereas there had only been two men standing guard against the whole wall of the forest she had been found in, here there were twelve men surrounding three separate but very closely erected tents.

Holofernes smiled at Judith. "This," he said, "is where we keep our treasure."

One of the men who saw Holofernes coming ordered the others to stand quickly at attention and salute their leader. Holofernes told them to stand down as he spoke softly to the guard in front of him. The man gave a gruff order and walked over to the smallest tent, where he pulled back the curtain. Carrying a torch handed to him by one of the guards, Holofernes pulled the entrance back, gave a slight bow, and ushered Judith in ahead of him.

As Judith's eyes adjusted to the dark, she saw before her a puzzling sight—though impressive, nonetheless. There in front of her was crate after crate, all locked and sealed. Around the crates, in greater number than she could count, were sacks tied with drawstrings. Holofernes kicked the first bag in front of him.

Judith's eyes widened as she saw the contents gleam in the torchlight. "Real treasure," she gasped, more to herself than Holofernes.

Holofernes heard her and laughed. "Yes, my lady. Every single crate and sack in here is filled with treasure just like this."

Judith had never seen so much gold in one place. The gold and silver coins shimmered in the soft light, and the few precious stones that had rolled onto the floor cast a light all around the room in a magnificent spectacle.

Judith looked up in amazement. "You have seized all of this in the short time you've been away?"

He smiled. "Three years is more than a short time. This, however, is only one of the tents we have. You saw the other two, which are bigger and more magnificent than this one. Each is filled to the brim with more gold and jewels than what any lord has ever owned."

Judith smiled at him. "Is this going to be handed out at the feast?"

"Some of it. Plenty will be taken back home, shared among the villagers, or used to build up our army to be even greater. I have had dreams," he continued, "of crossing the sea and taking the land to the east. I have had dreams of heading to the far north and defeating the barbaric tribes that live there. I want to take over their wild lands as well." He smiled proudly before he continued. "I have dreams of ruling the world, and this treasure is a mere fraction of the wealth that will be needed."

Judith smiled back at him. "With so many grand ideas, I am sure that you will achieve everything you want."

"Yes," he said, "I suppose I shall, and if I don't, I will keep on fighting until I have what I want. Fighting is in the blood of my men. As you can see, it is what we do best."

Judith gave a small sigh in understanding, but she couldn't help thinking to herself, *How in the world will I be able to defeat a man who claims the best thing he does is fight? And do I still want to defeat him? He seems like a good lord and a wise man, one who can be trusted by those who serve him.*

She looked down at the gold coins at her feet and thought about the life she could lead if she could convince Holofernes to return home and take her with him. In the dim light of the tent, the confused look on her face seemed to make her more radiant than ever.

"Tell me, my dear, what are you thinking about?" Holofernes asked.

She smiled at him and answered honestly. "I'm thinking about how I don't really have a home to return to. Will I ever be able to find a place to call home?"

Holofernes stared at her for a long time but remained silent.

Judith was looking at the coins at her feet, too timid to meet his eyes. Finally, Holofernes took one of Judith's delicate hands in his own rough, calloused one and led her back out into the sunlight as if the moment had never happened.

Holofernes made much ado about showing her the other two tents as well. Every single chest and bag was overflowing with treasure: gold, silver, coins, goblets, anything precious. Everything metal had been seized and saved. In the last tent there was a very small chest sitting on top of the rest. Holofernes went to it and picked it up. Inside were just a few items, and he selected the most beautiful one: it was a rare and ornate gold necklace. Three strands of thick gold were braided together, and a medallion of green sea glass hung from them. Judith had never seen anything so beautiful and regal in her life. As she touched the necklace ever so gently, it sparkled in the torchlight. The shimmer cast dancing shadows on the tent's walls, and she gasped at its elegance.

Holofernes looked at her again with that long, dark stare that seemed to see straight into her soul.

"I would like you to have this. Of everything we have found, this is the most beautiful. I would like to give it to the most beautiful woman I have ever met. Perhaps it can replace that wooden necklace of yours that seems so old and worn."

Judith's hand flew to her small necklace. She was terrified of losing it, but she didn't want to upset Holofernes. She bowed in appreciation. "My lord, nothing would please me more than to please you. It is a beautiful gift, but I cannot accept it."

Holofernes gave a soft laugh. He was so pleased with himself for his generosity that he seemed oblivious to Judith's worry.

"Wear it, my dear," he said, "and you will be safe here in the camp. Everyone will know that you are mine." After a moment of silence, he continued. "I have never taken a wife, even though my men believe I should have married long ago. But before I left my mother's hut, she shared an omen with me. She said, 'The woman who will have the greatest impact on your life will be beautiful beyond measure, and she will emerge unexpectedly from the woods. Hold her close to you, and do not let her out of your sight, for it is by her hand that your greatness will either rise or fall.' Now I think I know what her words meant. When our battle with Bethulia is over, my army and I will return home and bring you with us. You will become the queen you were meant to be."

The fire in Judith's heart burned brighter than ever. She was relieved that she had found a place where she seemed to belong, where she felt appreciated, and where, perhaps, she would be loved. She was honored by Holofernes's gesture, but still, she did not want to part with her old necklace.

"My lord," she said, "I don't know what to say. I am honored by your proposal and humbly accept it. I pray I can be the queen you and your people hope me to be."

"Then wear this token as a sign of our upcoming union. Allow me to help you remove that old string you have and replace it with something far better."

It was only then that Judith hesitantly spoke up. "My father made this for me. As I told you last night, I lost him long ago. This is the only gift I have from him."

At these words, Judith saw anger flash in Holofernes's eyes. She tensed, afraid of what would come next, but no sooner had the anger escaped his gaze than it was replaced by his usual, kind expression. *Perhaps I imagined it*, she thought. *The light in here is dim after all.*

Holofernes smiled warmly and said, "Come now, it is old and worn—not fit for a queen. Let's replace it with this."

With one more moment of hesitation, Judith finally removed her old necklace and allowed Holofernes to put on the new one. He let his hand linger on her neck and then travel up to caress her face. Judith could feel herself leaning into him and felt a sense of longing to be with him. Now it was Holofernes's turn to hesitate, but only for a moment. He also leaned in and let his thumb brush her lips. The air was tense with desire. In another moment, he drew her close and gave her the softest kiss she had ever received. It was short but sweet and filled with promise. Then he wrapped his great arms around her and kissed the crown of her head. When he finally pulled her back, Judith felt giddy. She was to become a queen and a wife. She smiled at the thought of it all, and Holofernes smiled back.

Without another word, Holofernes held out his hand for the old, worn-out string with the bird pendant. Entranced, Judith gave it to him graciously. Tears filled her eyes, and she hoped they were tears of happiness.

As Holofernes and Judith walked outside, Holofernes dropped the old necklace into the dirt without a moment's thought. He stepped right over it and continued on, leading Judith through the camp while he shared more stories of the battles he had won and the men who were so loyal to him.

Judith had trouble paying attention as he continued parading her about the camp. She spent the remainder of the afternoon in a rather confused emotional state. She made sure to coo and awe over all the great work the men had done, but her heart and head remained back in the tent.

The only distraction was when she and Holofernes spent some minutes listening to the scop. Holofernes introduced her to him as they were wrapping up their tour.

"I allowed this boy to join us three years ago. His parents were dead, and I threw his sister into a fire," Holofernes relayed with a laugh. Judith gasped at his words, which only made Holofernes laugh harder while the boy stared at his harp.

*Surely, he's joki*ng, she thought, but the boy's somber countenance sent an icy chill down her spine.

"Rowe has done well with us, and his magnificent voice has proven a valuable asset to boost morale," Holofernes continued when he had collected himself.

The scop was no more than thirteen years of age, and he was certainly not built to be a soldier. Judith noticed that he seemed grateful to be with Holofernes, but there was some hesitation.

Holofernes made him sing for them. The sweet melody transported Judith away from the camp and into a safe place where she felt calm and content for the first time in days. He smiled at her afterward, grateful that she appreciated the music. The music seemed to move Holofernes too, because just as the final notes trailed off, the great lord turned to Judith and invited her to dine with him once again.

She was pleased to receive the invitation but felt that she should not get too close to him so quickly. Instead of obliging, she said, "My lord, I would be honored, but my maid has been alone for a great while, and I must make sure that she is healing well. She has been quite weak and weary from our long journey. Perhaps you could allow me to spend the evening with her to keep her company."

Holofernes smiled in understanding. He, too, had a companion whom he looked after and frequently spent his time with. Old Beartwold was more than just an advisor, he was a friend. Unlike so many of the men who had watched Holofernes murder their lord, Beartwold admired the boy's tenacity. After the bloody fight, he'd taken the boy under his wing and trained him in the ways of his people. He was a strong and noble thane, and, along with Toland, had always been Holofernes's most trusted advisor.

Holofernes nodded. "Very well. I will see to it that food is brought to you for supper tonight. You are free to go back to your tent on your own. As long as you are wearing the necklace I gave you, my men will see that you are in my favor and will allow you to move about as you wish."

Judith looked up into Holofernes's eyes with a sincere look of appreciation and gratitude. "Thank you, my lord," she said. "Thank you for everything."

She took the great man's hand into hers and once again noticed how rough it was. Ever so carefully, she brought the back of his hand up to her lips and kissed it sweetly. She let go, bowed low to the ground, then headed back to Nerienda.

CHAPTER 13

Judith walked slowly back to her tent. She had a great deal to think about and was hoping to have some time alone to process everything that had just happened, but she did not get more than ten paces from Holofernes before someone grabbed her arm. Startled, she turned and saw Knut standing next to her with a look of suspicion on his face.

"Would you be so kind as to lead me back to my maid?" she asked innocently.

Knut gave a low grunt and trudged off in the direction of the tent, dragging Judith after him. He pulled at her arm so viciously that when he finally let go, she noticed a bruise where his hand had been, but she didn't dare complain. Having the army's largest and fiercest warrior watching her so closely was bad enough.

As they neared the tent, Knut let go, but the scowl on his face grew more intimidating. Judith looked bravely into his eyes, and her stare made him suspicious. He turned cautiously and slowly began to walk away. As soon as he rounded the corner, Judith scanned the area and saw that the guards had permitted Nerienda to go sit in the small clearing behind their tent. They immediately noticed Judith's gold necklace and gave a nod as she passed them on her way to her maid.

The old woman heard someone coming up behind her and turned quickly. When she saw it was Judith, she let out a small sigh of relief. Judith ran into her arms and stayed there for a few moments. Finally, Nerienda pulled away, looked into the maiden's face, and asked how the day had gone.

Judith sat back on her heels, wide-eyed with excitement. "Holofernes took me on a tour of the camp and introduced me to all of his officers and most loyal thanes."

Nerienda smiled at Judith. The girl seemed so excited that she was half expecting her to say she had figured out a master plan to solve all of their problems and they could go back to Bethulia that day. However, the conversation did not go as she had expected. Instead, Judith began telling her just how wise, strong, and courageous Holofernes was. Nerienda listened and, though she didn't say anything, she grew worried at how enamored Judith had become with Holofernes.

"Perhaps Holofernes is a good man after all. He wants the best for us," Judith said. "Just think, Nerienda. There is nothing left for us in Bethulia."

Nerienda could see the young woman was serious about leaving.

"What if," Judith continued, "we could convince Holofernes that it would be better for him to return home now and leave everyone in peace?"

Nerienda looked at Judith with concern. "Judith, you know what he has done to all of the towns between us and his home in the north. You saw the treasure he has amassed. It came at a price. Lives were lost to earn that. Women were hurt, children were orphaned, and probably even worse. You cannot seriously be thinking about running away with him?"

Judith looked at Nerienda. She wanted to tell her that she was only a maid and should do as she was told, but instead, all she could think to say was, "I don't think Holofernes is as bad as you think he is."

"Judith," Nerienda said, "think about the people you are abandoning. Even if Holofernes does turn and leave, it doesn't mean he won't come back or leave soldiers to fight after he is gone. Bethulia is already in ruins. People are starving. Children are ill. We must help them. That is why we were sent here."

"The people in Bethulia don't care about us! Cyneric sent us here knowing that we would likely be killed. The Bethulians only care about themselves, but we have the chance to run away and have a much better life. I could be a queen!"

As Judith spoke, her mind became clearer than it had been in days. She may have lost her father's necklace, but she could see what she was gaining in its place. For the moment, she felt the trade-off was a good one.

Nerienda understood that Holofernes had seriously changed Judith's opinion about the entire mission. She had sensed something was different, but it was not apparent until this moment just what was wrong. But then she saw it. Judith's bird necklace was gone.

"Where is your necklace?" she interrupted.

Her alarm stopped Judith mid-sentence. "I... this was a gift from Holofernes." Her excitement faded. It was much easier to reconcile the loss of the necklace when she didn't have to discuss it. As she thought about what happened, tears suddenly formed in her eyes.

"When Holofernes gave me this one," she said as she pointed to her neck, "he had me take my old one off and give it to him, but he didn't keep it. He just threw it on the ground."

Nerienda watched the girl closely. "Do you remember where

he left it?"

"I do. It was just outside the tents filled with treasure."

Nerienda nodded. She knew that the only way to convince Judith that her new plan would lead to devastating consequences was to go back for the necklace and get her to reconnect with her past.

"Good," she said. "We will go get it back for you."

Judith looked at Nerienda with a puzzled expression, but it seemed so important to the maid that she nodded in agreement.

"That will be easy," Judith said. "Now that I wear this necklace, we are permitted to move about camp as we like."

Nerienda narrowed her eyes. "We might be able to walk around, but I've no doubt suspicious behavior will still be reported… and punished. We will go tonight after the sun has set," Nerienda continued as she thought aloud. "The feast is not until tomorrow, but the men will be preoccupied with preparations, and we should have no trouble walking about unnoticed."

With their guards watching carefully from a distance, they sat in the meadow for a while longer, looking out into the woods. The day had been a whirlwind of ups and downs. Judith felt she had experienced every emotion within only a few hours, and she was tired and weary. Nerienda sat on a fallen log, and Judith laid her head in her lap and dozed as she had so often done as a little girl. Finally, at sunset, Nerienda shook Judith awake and beckoned the girl to follow her back to their tent. They returned only moments before dinner was served, and they ate in silence as they contemplated their new plans.

CHAPTER 14

It wasn't long before darkness settled, and when it did, Judith and Nerienda stepped out of the tent. The same two guards were on watch with orders to make sure the women stayed close to the tent, but when they saw Judith's necklace, they allowed them to pass by without question.

With bonfires lit, torches burning, and small campfires scattered around the army camp, Judith carefully led Nerienda through the tents. While they were meandering, a few men made comments here and there, but for the most part, nobody bothered them. In the firelight, Judith's necklace glistened with a regal radiance, and the men allowed them to pass by. All the men had heard word of Holofernes's promise about making Judith his queen. They knew better than to stir up any trouble as everyone knew the feast was when the lord gifted his treasures to those who were in his favor.

Judith and Nerienda proceeded slowly since Nerienda was still supposed to be recovering from her injury. Judith had walked their path a few times, and she felt fairly comfortable with it, but once or twice she found herself lost among the sea of tents. However, she did not dare ask anyone for directions, as she didn't want to raise suspicion.

Despite having to circle back a few times, they finally made their way to the corner tents that had been guarded by twelve thanes during the day. When they arrived, though, Judith noticed there were now only six men on watch. It seemed that with all the feast preparations underway and no fear of threat to the camp, a smaller number of guards was assigned to the post.

The thanes were sitting around a campfire, speaking to each other in excited tones. Judith could hear their whispers and knew they were discussing the feast. She carefully tucked her necklace under her dress and veil so that it didn't shimmer in the firelight. Slowly, she and Nerienda crept around the tents and over to the area where her bird necklace had been dropped. Ducking into the shadows, they crouched down on the ground and began feeling around in the dirt. After several minutes of searching, both women began to grow anxious. The necklace was nowhere to be found. During the day, it must have been kicked around by the foot traffic. Despite the danger, they had to spread out.

It wasn't until they reached the smallest tent that they finally found the little bird in the folds of the animal hides where the tent met the ground. Nerienda picked it up quietly, put it in her pocket, and whispered to the girl that it was time to return to their tent, but Judith didn't want to leave just yet.

"Quick, Nerienda, come inside," she whispered. "Let me show you all the beautiful treasure they have here."

Judith pulled Nerienda into the tent before the old woman could object. As they slipped inside, Judith quickly grabbed the nearest torch and took it in with them. Once the tent's opening was secured, the two women stood side by side, looking over the crates and bags. Nerienda stood silently, stunned at the amount of wealth that had been pillaged. Judith kicked the same bag Holofernes had earlier, and even more gold and jewels spilled out.

"Look, Nerienda, not only could I be queen, but I could be the richest queen in the country."

Nerienda looked at Judith with pursed lips. She was incredibly worried about her charge. The two began walking through the tent. They found more crates and chests than they could count. They opened a few of them and found more gold, coins, jewels, even goblets, all made of precious metals and stones. Finally, just when they were getting ready to leave, something caught Nerienda's eye in the far corner.

"Judith," she whispered, "what's over there?"

"Oh, just more gold, I am sure," Judith replied.

But Nerienda was insistent. "No. There is something else. Something strange."

Judith walked over slowly with the torch in hand. When she got close enough, she was able to cast a light into the corner, and there, amongst the folds of the canvas and animal hides, was a small pile of pots, dishes, work tools, and clothing. The pots were sturdy and of good use. The clay dishes had a few chips and cracks, but nothing that couldn't be mended. The other metal goods needed a decent wash, but otherwise everything seemed to be in working order. Curiosity got the better of them, and they continued to sort through the odds and ends for a long while, losing track of time.

As they were nearing the bottom of the pile, they found some beautiful fabric amongst several ordinary blankets, a few bags of wool, and several pieces of practical clothing. Nerienda inspected the items with growing interest but suddenly let out a sharp gasp. Her eyes widened, and the hair on her neck stood straight up. Judith looked over to her, afraid that the woman had been bitten by an animal. Instead, she saw tears in her eyes as she held up an object Judith could barely make out in the dim light.

Judith took the object from Nerienda and held it closer to her face. She immediately recognized what she was holding, and her eyes widened too as a small cry of surprise escaped her lips. There before her was a small rag doll, not much more than a few pieces of fabric and coarse wool fibers, with her hair and dress torn. One eye was missing, but the other was made from something unusual. *Was it a garnet?* She recognized it from the ones that hung on her own necklace, but this one was much smaller and darker. *Peculiar*, she thought.

Judith looked at Nerienda. "It's nothing. Just a doll that was left behind," she said.

Nerienda looked at her, concerned the girl could not see the reality that was staring her in the face. Nerienda studied the doll carefully. It was the only toy they had come across, and something about it did not sit well with her. She too noticed the garnet and recognized the gem immediately.

"Judith," Nerienda said, "this doll belonged to a child. A child who doesn't need it anymore." Her voice trembled, and she hoped she didn't have to explain any further.

Judith looked at her. "Perhaps they are just saving it and will return it once the battles have calmed down."

Nerienda shook her head. "These men do not care about anyone but themselves. The people who wore these clothes are gone. The people who needed these tools and pots do not need them anymore because they are no longer alive. And the child who owned this... you can be certain she was murdered with all the rest, Judith. These men are savages, barbarians, and monsters who want nothing more than to take over the whole country and rule it all. They are not merciful. Holofernes may be smart and strategic, but he is not a kind or just lord. Tell me… does Holofernes act with mercy?"

Judith thought back to the story at lunch, how unbothered he'd been by killing the goat, and the way he'd laughed about throwing Rowe's sister into a fire. The realization of everything around her set in as her eyes rested on the doll lying in her lap. Finally, her thoughts settled on the fact that Holofernes had so unceremoniously thrown her necklace aside, despite the reminder of how important it was to her. As she sat in the darkness, she began to shake.

Judith cried for the little girl who lost this doll. She was afraid to dwell on what might have happened to her and the other children whose families had resisted the army. Nerienda held her for a long time as the two sat in the corner of the tent mourning the loss of the lives of all those people. The jewels no longer seemed as beautiful. Instead, they seemed dull and lifeless, stained with blood.

Nerienda suddenly heard footsteps outside the tent and hushed the girl. After the footsteps circled the tent several times, the entrance was pulled back, and someone stepped inside.

The two women held their breath and hid the torch in the corner behind the crates so that not even a shadow could be seen from where the guard stood. If they were discovered, the odds of completing their mission would diminish. They probably wouldn't even live to see the morning.

They crouched low, and they could hear the footsteps moving about. A man yelled something in a language they weren't familiar with. Someone responded and quickly came over to the tent.

One of Holofernes's clever war tactics was that he taught the men of his inner circle his Celtic language. It allowed them to speak to each other in secret when others were present. When any thane grew suspicious, they switched to the Celtic language Holofernes had grown up with.

The two guards exchanged a few more words that the women could not understand. One of them stepped forward, opened some of the crates, lifted a couple of the bags and put them back down. The women could tell by the sounds that the men were cleaning up the mess that Holofernes made when he had kicked the bag open earlier. Both men were breathing heavily, which reassured Judith that it would be nearly impossible for them to hear her and Nerienda.

Once the cleanup was done, the two men shared more whispered words and scanned the tent one more time. Then without further inspection, they walked back out into the night. Just as the tent door was closing, one of the men asked, "Where's the torch? I thought we left it here earlier."

"Wulfstan must have taken it again," the other one replied. "He's always taking it when he wanders off for a piss. Why the man can't piss in the dark like a normal soldier I will never understand. It seems like it's more trouble to take it with you, really."

The two men laughed and wandered off. As soon as their voices became distant, Judith and Nerienda moved to the tent entrance. Nerienda peeked outside, pulling back the curtain ever so slightly. When the coast was clear, she stepped outside and motioned for Judith to follow her. They put the torch back in its place and rounded the corner toward the dark forest.

The women moved about the perimeter of the camp just on the forest's edge. Judith made sure that her necklace was well hidden so as not to reflect the moon, the stars, or the firelight. It took time to circle the camp. They walked slowly, careful to step over twigs and branches, trying to make as little sound as possible. Judith was mindful of the hiding spots around her and was ready should they run into a hungry animal. The fresh meat that was being roasted certainly smelled like something a hungry wolf would be waiting in the shadows to seize. As they walked, Judith took out the small blade that the blacksmith had given her.

The camp seemed quiet in the late-night hours. Finally, they reached the small clearing behind their tent, and the two women raced back to safety. They slowed down as they rounded the corner of their tent. The same two guards stood waiting for them. When she saw the men, Judith became worried, but Nerienda was calm and collected. She looked at each of the guards square in the face and gave a pleasant smile.

"Good night, gentlemen," she said. "We are very tired after all the excitement of the past few days and do not wish to be disturbed until morning."

The men nodded without question.

Judith and Nerienda crawled back into their tent and collapsed in the corner. After she caught her breath, Nerienda pulled the doll out from the folds of her dress and placed it in Judith's lap. Then she took the necklace from her pocket and placed it in Judith's palm, closing the maiden's fingers around it. Judith burst into tears at the sight of both and wept for a long while. She was careful to stifle her cries so the guards could not hear her sobs. Finally, when Judith calmed down enough to think more clearly, Nerienda offered her a few sips of the mead left over from dinner.

"What are we going to do?" Judith whispered.

Nerienda looked at Judith's tear-soaked face. The old woman tried to give a comforting smile, but she, too, was struggling. Holofernes and his men were savage dogs, and it pained her to know that Judith had wanted so badly to be a part of their community. But once again she refrained from saying anything that would hurt Judith further.

Nerienda whispered, "Well, we still have time until the feast."

Judith's brow furrowed with a deep crease, unsure of what the maid was talking about.

"When you told me Holofernes's story," Nerienda continued, "you mentioned that the lord had watched him to find out what his weaknesses were. We have one day to do the same."

Judith voiced her concern. "But he's such a strong man. He certainly doesn't have any weaknesses."

Nerienda shook her head. "There is always something. We must discover his and use it to our advantage. To be honest, I'm almost sure you are one of his weaknesses, which is to our benefit."

Judith opened her mouth to protest, but Nerienda continued.

"Now is not the time to be modest, Judith. You have managed to convince him in the span of less than two days that you are not only harmless, but worthy of being his queen. Tomorrow you must find a reason to spend time with him again. Perhaps we both can."

"But he is a monster," Judith blurted out as she thought back to how Holofernes had tricked her into trusting him. Not only had he pretended to be kind and gentle, but he'd said he cared for her—all the while boasting about his conquests and the riches he'd amassed from innocent people he'd murdered in cold blood.

"I do not wish to spend one more second in his company."

Nerienda felt as if a weight had been lifted from her weary shoulders. *Finally, she is learning,* she thought to herself. She gave a nod of approval.

"Of course you do not want to be around him. No one in their right mind would if they knew the things we know, but this is what we came to do. Now the real work must begin. Tomorrow we must take the time to learn as much as we can about our adversary, and then we'll wait for the perfect moment to attack."

CHAPTER 15

Judith fell asleep with tears in her eyes as she held the doll tightly in one hand and her little bird in the other. Her sleep was restless, and she awoke several times throughout the night. She found herself tossing and turning, and every sound outside the tent startled her. Despite the quiet stillness of only a few hours earlier, now it seemed that she and Nerienda were the only two in the entire camp who were trying to sleep. Everyone else was making a final push to get everything ready for the feast. There was much to be done, and work continued throughout the night.

In the early hours before dawn, Judith heard the men outside her tent running back and forth, shouting orders to each other in excitement. Most of these men had lived on squirrels and rabbits for the last several months and were excited to finally fill their bellies past full. Every one of them planned to gorge on the meat and to drink more mead than they had seen in all three years of their travels and fighting.

Judith lay on her cot with Nerienda's words echoing in her heart: *Now the real work must begin.* She was anxious, but the anxiety stemmed from the fear that, up until now, her actions may have hindered their progress. She had been such a fool to believe

Holofernes could be a good man. She had allowed his charm to cloud her vision of their mission, and most embarrassingly, she had ignorantly delighted in the idea of being his queen. *Stupid girl*, she found herself saying, over and over. *What were you thinking?*

As her panic cooled and her mind cleared, she finally realized what the real problem was—that she just hadn't been thinking. These past few days she had only been observing and reacting. *Still, my actions haven't been detrimental yet, and perhaps they can be used to our advantage.*

Cyneric had ordered her to do whatever was necessary to succeed in her mission. The first task was endearing herself to this beastly man. Her demeanor these past few days was exactly what was needed to gain the lord's trust. Her reactions had been genuine, and precisely because of this, their plan might just work. She had done everything exactly right—apart from letting her heart get swept up into the mess, but there was no time to go back and fix that. Now it was time to implement the second part of her plan. The details were still hazy, but the outcome was certain. *Holofernes must die soon, or all will be lost.*

Judith realized she had been playing absentmindedly with the little bird that she still held between her fingers. Her favorite part of the carving was that no matter which way you looked at it, the bird on the front and the one on the back were always flying in opposite directions. This inconsequential detail had become quite meaningful to her over the years. She had always longed to be like a bird, to flap her wings and fly off past the horizon in any direction she chose without city walls to hold her back.

Now Judith was well beyond the gates of the city. Instead of feeling free and liberated, she felt anxious and afraid, but as her hand rested on her necklace, she found a certain peace. She remembered the gifts of her God to the prophets, lords, leaders, and other men and women called to do great things. She thought back to the stories her father had told her growing up: Daniel in the lion's den, David and Goliath, Jonah and the Leviathan… all men who should have failed in their missions. But when everything and everyone else had failed, God chose these unassuming characters. Daniel might have been a visionary, but never a lion tamer. David was a mere shepherd, not even special among his brothers. Jonah was an unwilling participant in aiding Nineveh… thus, the whale swallowed him. Even with that major obstacle hindering him, he was still able to carry out his mission.

Judith lay in the dark tent and began to understand. It was not the size nor the courage of those God had chosen, but their willingness to say yes to God's calling. She might be just one small person, but her God was great and all-powerful. If He desired to work through her to liberate her people, Judith felt ready.

Exhausted, but with her fears calmed, Judith finally managed to doze off. She was awoken shortly after by the noises outside, and so she resigned herself to getting up. Dawn was beginning to break anyway, and there was much to do. Outside the tent, she noticed that two new guards had taken the place of the men from the night before. When they looked at her, she smiled politely and went to sit on a tree stump beside the tent.

CHAPTER 16

The sun was just peeking over the treetops, but the air was already buzzing with anticipation as the heartbeat of the camp thumped to a rhythmic, festive drum. Everyone seemed full of gaiety. Everyone except Judith. While the rest of the camp ran about in a frenzy, she sat still—watching and waiting.

She had a clear vantage point to observe the soldiers running around preparing for the celebration. One man passed the tent carrying Holofernes's armor. Another carried a sack of onions over his shoulder, while two others meandered past carrying a large cart of firewood for the bonfire. She watched the army's foreign world pass in front of her, and she heard voices shouting jovially as orders were sent out to all corners of the camp.

"Unfearth, how may goats have been butchered? What? That's not enough, we need at least a dozen more."

"Wulf, open the largest barrels of mead—we cannot have too much of it tonight."

"Godric, more wood for the fire. Hurry."

"Byrtwold, polish our lord's armor till it shines. Tonight, he is to look like the great ruler he is."

The commands continued as the preparations were finalized and the hour of the feast drew closer.

Judith spent her time thinking and wondering just what the day would bring with a new resolve to carry out her mission. She knew she had to be mindful of everything that unfolded around her, especially with regard to Holofernes. She sat for a long while thinking about the man, his deep eyes, and his muscular frame. She tried to imagine what, if anything, might be his weakness besides her.

Truthfully, it took some time for her to see how she could be a weakness. Eventually, she realized that just like the rest of the men, Holofernes had not seen a beautiful woman in years, at least not one that he did not have the intention of killing immediately. She could use her beauty to her advantage. Holofernes seemed to be relaxed in her company. She had noticed that Toland took great care to make sure Holofernes did not do or say anything foolish around her, and yet the great lord still seemed to occasionally let things slip that he would not normally tell outsiders.

Judith was keenly aware of the desire that burned in Holofernes's eyes when he looked at her. At first, this passion had excited her. But now she knew she would have a hard time looking him in the eye knowing what she knew about him. Still, if she was going to complete her mission, she would have to pretend to be as enamored with him as he was with her.

The sun was beginning to rise, and the guards were chatting about the feast. Judith sat just within earshot.

"But of course," one of the guards said, "none of us likes mead quite as much as our great lord."

Both men laughed at the remark. Judith's ears perked up. She was careful not to say a word or stir from her tree stump. Instead, she stayed quiet and watched the sun rise into the sky.

Nerienda soon woke up and called to her. Judith looked in on her, smiled, and went back into the tent. A few minutes later, the guards brought breakfast. It was a bit more decadent than the meal from the previous day, a small portion of food from the feast that was to come, and it proved to be far more delicious than anything they had tasted in recent months. The meat was juicy, the potatoes were earthy, and the cabbage had been cooked down sweetly. However, the mead was far and away the most delicious item on the menu. It was strong and rich, and it flowed down their throats like honey that warmed them from the inside. Judith understood why Holofernes and the men were looking forward to the drink so much. It was easily the best mead she'd ever tasted.

When they were done, she felt a bit more refreshed. Nerienda looked at her and laughed.

"My dear," she said, "we must get you ready for the day. You look like you slept terribly, and we don't want the great lord to think that you are not enjoying his accommodations."

Judith nodded in agreement and allowed Nerienda to set to work fixing her makeup. With a few quick touches, Nerienda was able to open up Judith's eyes to make her look more awake. She also added some color to her cheeks to hide the girl's pallor. Finally, she gave a touch of pink to Judith's lips. Soon, the maiden in front of her looked radiant once again.

When they were done, the two women sat in the tent, and Judith shared her early morning ideas with Nerienda. She told her that Holofernes might have a weakness for mead. Nerienda listened carefully, happy to see that the girl was finally back to planning their original mission. They talked for quite some time, and when Toland finally entered the tent and beckoned Judith to go with him, it was already nearing midday.

"Would it be alright," Judith asked, "if Nerienda came with me?

She has been cooped up in this tent for two days and is finally feeling better. I'm sure she would love to see the feast preparations today just as much as I do."

Toland looked at Nerienda then back at Judith. He seemed to be pondering the question for a few long moments before finally saying, "Very well, but she stays right next to you. Neither of you are to wander away from where you are supposed to be. I will be watching you closely. There is too much going on, and if you get in the way, you might ruin the feast."

"Of course," Judith said. "We do not want to interfere in any way."

He led the two women out into the bright sunlight and off, once again, toward the center of camp. Holofernes was sitting as usual in the great tent next to his own personal quarters. When they arrived, he was hungrily eating his breakfast. The meal looked very similar to their own, only with double portions. Judith could see he was enjoying his mead as well, just as the guards had joked. There was a full pitcher sitting next to his table in addition to the goblet that he drank from. Whatever battle tactics he and Toland had gone over that morning had already been discussed. Judith made a mental note that the meetings, like the one she had interrupted the first morning, seemed to be conducted in the early morning hours. *This is why we are not called to see him until much later in the day,* she thought.

There was so much commotion around the tent that the lord did not notice the women walk in. However, when Toland cleared his throat, Holofernes looked up from his food, noticed his guests, and gave a broad smile through a mouthful of mutton. He jumped up to greet them, accidentally spilling the mead from his cup. He walked over to the two women, beaming with excitement.

"Good morning, dear ladies. It is nearly time for the feast. As you can see, all is going well and at dusk the celebration will begin."

Despite her disgust at the grease dripping down Holofernes's chin into his stubbled beard, Judith forced herself to smile. Desperately trying to match her excitement to his, she said, "It looks like it will be absolutely wonderful, a great feast, truly."

Nerienda, however, did not say anything. It was the first time she had been out in the camp in the daylight, and she just stood where she was with her mouth agape as she stared at everything before her: the elaborate table, the huge tent that had been erected, the bonfires all around, the smells of delicious food, and the barrels of strong drink. All of it absolutely overwhelmed her. She could not believe the craftsmanship, skill, and care that went into everything that had been done.

Holofernes studied Nerienda, waiting for her to say something. When she remained silent, he became a bit disgruntled. The smile on his face disappeared and was replaced by a stern scowl. Nerienda didn't notice the lord's change in demeanor, but Judith was acutely aware of it.

"Forgive her, my lord," she said quickly. "Nerienda is not used to seeing such elaborate preparations taking place. She is truly as astounded as I am."

Hearing her name, Nerienda looked up and realized her mistake. "I beg your pardon, my lord. I did not mean to offend you, I am simply marveling at everything that is before me. The tent that your men have built is gigantic. This table… I've never seen craftsmanship at this level. The bonfires and the sheer amount of wood it took to build them are impressive. This is an absolutely incredible endeavor. I applaud you and your men for such magnificent work."

Nerienda's truthful words satiated Holofernes's large ego. He looked down on her with a broad, greasy smile and said, "My brave men are the absolute best at everything. That is why they are my men."

"Indeed," Nerienda said. "I can see that."

"They are the best at everything because they have their great lord to lead them," Judith added with a smile.

Holofernes turned his attention back to her, and his smile spread even wider.

The day was going to be a beautiful one. Judith was even a bit disappointed she wouldn't be invited to the feast. Holofernes seemed to read her mind.

"My dear," he began, "sadly, my men forbid outsiders be allowed to our feast. It is simply against their rules. However, I encourage you to walk about today. Talk with the men and enjoy the food. When you are done, relax and rest, and I will see you in the morning. I have spoken with my advisors and there is much for you and me to discuss. We look forward to you and your maid traveling with us on the rest of our journey."

Judith smiled politely, but Holofernes's words had caused a surge of panic within her. She knew that this feast was a time when everyone let their guard down, and therefore the perfect opportunity to strike. If she waited to see Holofernes again until morning, she might miss her chance. So, gathering up her courage, she looked at Holofernes sweetly. Then, despite the large number of men around them, she stepped a bit closer to the lord and stood on her toes as she leaned toward his ear.

Understanding that she wanted to tell him something privately, he bent low so that her lips brushed the side of his face.

"Forgive my boldness, my lord," Judith said in barely a whisper, "but you have given me so much, it would be an honor if I could show you my gratitude tonight alone after the feast."

Knowing that this was a bold move, Judith immediately cast her eyes down to the ground and did not dare look at Holofernes, who stood shocked. Never had he heard of a woman saying such words to any man. However, he also knew Judith was no ordinary woman and found her boldness endearing. In the past few days, she had managed to surprise him more than any woman or man he had ever known, and he loved her for it. Only a woman with such qualities was good enough to be his wife, and her request amused and delighted him.

Slowly, he tilted her chin up until her eyes were staring back into his. Despite all the commotion around them, it seemed to both Judith and Holofernes that they were the only two people in the entire world at that moment… but each felt this for very different reasons. Both hearts pounded, both minds swirled with excitement, and both eyes conveyed an earnestness that could not be mistaken.

Holofernes nodded and said, "I would like that very much. I will see you tonight, my queen."

"Thank you, my lord," Judith answered as she bowed again. Then the two women quickly hurried off, careful to avoid Toland's menacing stare.

Once the women were out of the lord's sight, Nerienda whispered, "What did you say to him?"

"I said that I wanted to show my gratitude to him in private tonight."

Nerienda's hand flew to her mouth, but a gasp still managed to escape. It was unthinkable for any woman to be so forward with a man. For her sweet Judith to be so audacious with a terrible warlord was beyond anything she could have imagined only three days before. Judith looked at her and then looked down at the ground. After a few paces, she looked back at her maid and started to laugh. Nerienda had to laugh at the absurdity of the situation too. Never in a million years did she think this was how their plan was going to play out. One of Holofernes's weaknesses was Judith. The other was mead. Judith and Nerienda realized that the crazy proposition might, in fact, be the best possible scenario for them.

They had just walked past the area where the food was being prepared. It smelled divine, and one of the cooks offered the women a generous portion of leg of lamb. The women decided to walk the perimeter in a full circle as best they could. They needed to reestablish their bearings if they were going to be out again in the dark. Without the sun to guide them, the camp easily turned into a maze, and they could not afford to get lost making their escape. They needed to be sure they had a straight path home.

They noticed that the guard duty had been relaxed. Only a few men stood on the outskirts, and none of them seemed to be bothering with any sort of lookout except the guards toward the south, where Bethulia was located. They also observed that the guards who stood on the perimeter's edge on the east, their friends Acwel and Aart, slacked off greatly during their watch, either taking naps or sitting on some stump talking to one another. At other posts, the guards carried cups of mead in their hands.

Judith and Nerienda ambled around the large perimeter of the camp three times, making sure they understood exactly where everything was. The grand tent where the feast was being held was exactly in the center, and Holofernes's quarters were just off to the side of it. There was no clear-cut path straight down the center of camp toward the open clearing—it would have been far too noticeable anyway. Instead, they decided that the best route would be from Holofernes's tent past several smaller tents branching out to the east. They would pass ten tents total: Holofernes's on the left, two on the right, one on the left, two more on the right, and three on the left with one final tent to the right. It was not a straight line, but it was the shortest. There was only a mere five yards between the last two tents and the forest's edge.

Once they got to the edge of the forest, they needed to turn south and walk along the perimeter carefully so as not to rouse any suspicion. They also noticed the camp's guards always stood at the same posts no matter the hour, but they hoped that tonight there would be even fewer guards around.

From the wooded forest, they would march south as quickly and quietly as they could. When the forest ended and the city gate was clearly visible, they planned to run full speed down the meadow and up to the gate. They hoped and prayed that the guards on the outskirts of the camp would be too busy enjoying the feast to notice them, and once they were halfway to the city gates, they knew they would be too far away for any of the well-fed, inebriated men to catch them.

There was one more thing they needed to discuss, and Judith could not put off the issue any longer. Finally, she asked, "How exactly am I supposed to kill Holofernes? I certainly can't do it with strength."

"No, you're right. There is nothing you could do that would beat him in battle, but you do have the upper hand when it comes to cunning and craftiness. He sees you as a very innocent maiden." Nerienda paused for a moment and took out her handkerchief. Stooping low, she used it to pick up some nightshade leaves. "I think the best thing we can do is poison him."

"Yes, it seems like the only logical option," Judith replied.

Nerienda smiled. "Your biggest challenge will be to convince Holofernes to drink the poison. But as much as he seems to trust you, I don't think that will be an issue."

Judith wasn't nearly as convinced. Even when Holofernes had his guard down, his loyal thanes did not. Judith shook her head. "I don't think I'll be able to simply walk into Holofernes's tent with a cup for him to drink."

"No, but you are more than welcome to walk into Holofernes's quarters and request a drink for yourself," Nerienda answered. "And then you could slip the poison into his drink once you are alone with him."

The old woman tucked the nightshade neatly under her apron before crouching low to pick up a few poisonous mushrooms.

Judith considered her options. "And what would we put the poison in? I couldn't very well carry it in my hand."

The maid agreed, but after a few moments, her face lit up. "Quickly, come with me," she commanded.

The two walked the long perimeter back to their tent, making sure they were giving nods of greeting and warm smiles to everyone they met. The men were so excited about the upcoming feast, they barely gave the women any notice.

CHAPTER 17

When they got back to their tent, Nerienda asked the guards to light a fire for them even though the day was unseasonably warm. Ham, the younger of the two, looked at her questioningly, but Nerienda only laughed.

"These old bones could give me a chill on a summer's day at noon. If you would be so kind as to start a fire for me, I would truly appreciate it. Around the back would be preferred," she continued, "that way I won't get trampled by the passing men in their preparations for tonight."

Ham, still uncertain, looked to his mate, Wallis, for orders. His companion just nodded and sent him on his way to build the fire. Nerienda and Judith crept into their tent, where they found a few pieces of bread and two small cups of mead waiting for them.

Once the tent's entrance was secure, Nerienda went over to the bag they had brought with them on the journey. She pulled everything out, looked it over, and then laid it aside. Finally, she pulled out a small vial. It had perfume in it, a sweet scent Judith had never worn, but one she had been given as a gift from her father. The vial was quite small and only contained enough of the decadent scent for two or three uses. Nerienda uncorked it and splashed Judith with its entire contents, hitting both her face and neck. Judith coughed as the strong odor swirled around her.

"What are you doing?" Her eyes stung and watered.

Without answering, Nerienda went over to their wash bowl, dipped the vial in a few times and rinsed it out.

"Now we need to roast the nightshade leaves and the poisonous mushrooms. Once they are charred and brittle, we will grind them up into a fine powder. Then the powder goes into this vial. You will add the vial's contents to Holofernes's drink and then mix it around ever so slightly. If he doesn't have a drink with him, it is your job to make sure he gets one. If you can pour all the powder in his mug, there will be enough poison in his drink to stop his heart after only one good gulp. Then our job will be done, and we can head home."

Judith listened intently, careful to memorize every instruction. The part that seemed most dangerous to her was roasting the plants over the fire. Everything else could be attempted in secret.

"How will we keep the guards from disturbing us while the plants cook?"

"That is where you come in," Nerienda continued. "I will sit by the fire and make sure that everything is cooked. We only need a slight char—anything burnt will be useless. It won't take long. In the meantime, you must stay with the guards. Ask as many questions as you dare. Keep them occupied and make them forget that I'm even around."

Judith didn't have time to respond before Ham poked his head into the tent.

"The fire is ready, ladies. You are welcome to come out anytime."

After he'd gone, Nerienda took one last look at Judith, gathered up the nightshade and mushrooms, tucked them under her apron, and walked out to the fire.

Ham followed Nerienda around the back of the tent and waited until she settled herself on an old log. He looked at her and asked if there was anything else she needed. With as much appreciation as she could muster, she said, "Oh, thank you, but no. I am fine here. I just need to rest and warm myself."

"Of course," the young man said, but he continued to look at Nerienda.

Nerienda was beginning to grow uneasy and wasn't sure how to get rid of him. Finally, she suggested, "I believe Judith has some questions for you. Would you mind going to assist her? Don't worry about me, I'll be just fine here."

The guard looked at her again, and though he hesitated to leave, the proposition was a good one. He could either stay with an old woman, who was comfortably sitting in front of the fire, or go back to the young and beautiful maiden who wanted to spend time talking with him.

There was a moment of hesitation, but the thane bowed his head and said, "If you need anything at all, simply give a yell, and we will be right here."

"Of course," Nerienda said. "Thank you."

The guard rounded the corner of the tent and hurried to speak with Judith. She was still inside, unsure of what to do or say, when Ham poked his head in without ceremony.

"My lady," he said, "you sent for me?"

At first Judith had no idea what he was talking about, but she quickly realized Nerienda must have sent him to her so she could roast the plants.

"Oh, yes," she said without missing a beat, "I have so many questions I have been waiting to ask. Do you have a moment to speak with me?"

Ham smiled at her. "Of course. Would you be so kind as to come outside so we can have a proper conversation? I am not permitted to remain long in your tent."

Judith laughed sweetly. "I will be right there. I only need a moment." She watched the young man exit and took only a second to fall to her knees to say a quick prayer. Then she stood up to her full height, drew in a deep breath, adjusted her veil, and took one final sip from her mead cup. She spread down the folds of her skirt and then marched out of the tent, confident and proud.

As the bright sunshine hit Judith, she instantly grew anxious. It was easy to feign confidence in the shadows of a tent, but it felt as if the sunlight exposed all her insecurities. She could smell the fire burning behind the tent, and she caught the lightest scent of Nerienda's roasted vegetation. It wasn't enough to alarm the guards, though. As the scent reached her nose, she realized there was no turning back. She must succeed, or Nerienda would be found out. She looked at the guards, who seemed eager for her to join them.

"Beautiful day, isn't it?" she said as she approached them.

"Indeed, it is. A perfect day for a feast," Ham replied.

"Oh, the feast! Tell me," she asked, "what happens at Holofernes's feasts?"

The young man gave a slight grin. "They are the most wonderful part about being a thane to our lord. He is known far and wide for his feasts. They are almost as impressive as the battles he has won." The guard let out a soft laugh, amused with his own wit.

"I have only ever been to a handful of feasts," Judith replied. "I know they all have good food, drink, and music, but each one is always a bit different from the rest. Tell me, what happens at yours?"

Ham continued without giving a second thought to her question.

"Holofernes does not give many feasts, but when he does, there is always lots of food and strong drink. Everyone gets more than their share, and you can even take some back to the tent for the morning if you'd like. The food is just as good at first light as it is when served warm. Holofernes also has a way of finding the best mead from other towns and villages, and this is shared amongst everyone equally."

Judith had wondered why the mead she had earlier that day had tasted so unique. It was because it had come from a far corner of the country she had never heard of.

"I had some earlier. It was very sweet," she mused. "Quite delicious."

"That's the danger of it," Ham replied. "You barely notice how much you've had, and the next thing you know you can't count the number of fingers on your hand."

Best to limit myself then, Judith thought.

As if he was reading her mind, Ham added, "But there are no limits at a feast. Every man eats until he can't eat any more and drinks until he has passed out drunk."

"Is that all you do? Eat and drink?"

"Oh, no. After everyone has eaten and the mead is still flowing, the scop comes up to sing. Holofernes has found the best one we've ever heard. Rowe is only a boy, but he can sing a song more beautifully than an angel."

"I've heard him. He is extremely talented," Judith replied.

"He has a knack for telling stories. He knows each of us by name, and he always manages to weave in the names of every man in the army. Holofernes is always sung about as the greatest lord in the land, and his advisors are the wisest. The thanes are always the bravest and fight most heroically. The boy can tell a story, that's for sure!

"He can play melodies and harmonies on his harp that no one has ever heard before. Sometimes we wonder if he is really as young as he says he is. It seems he'd need a lot more time to develop his skills. A few of us have a theory that he lies about his age because that keeps him from having to fight in the battles. Although he tells great stories of heroics, he is a coward, always hiding when we go off to fight. Whenever we return in victory, we find him having pissed himself in some tent off in a dark corner of camp. The poor lad can't even stand to hear a war cry before his knees start shaking."

Judith imagined what it would be like to be that young boy, to have your home destroyed, and then be taken captive by the men who killed your loved ones and forced to sing songs of their bravery and great deeds. She knew she would be scared too.

For a brief moment she allowed herself to imagine what would happen if she failed in her efforts to kill Holofernes. She remembered the black smoke that filled the sky the night Godwine died and imagined Bethulia in flames. She could hear the people she knew so intimately screaming, and her heart suddenly ached for them. She saw the boys she grew up with, now men, dead on the battlefield, Cyneric too, and tears began to well up as she thought of Ellette being dealt a fate like Rowe's sister.

I didn't realize how much I love them. Dear God, forgive me. I cannot fail. Help me save my people. Judith suddenly remembered where she was and snapped back to the present.

"What happens after the boy is done singing?" she finally asked, realizing that she had let a moment of silence linger just a little too long.

Ham seemed not to have noticed the lull. "He can go on for quite some time, but his voice is so beautiful no one ever minds. Once he is done, the best part of the feast begins... Holofernes presents us with gifts."

"Gifts?" Judith asked.

"Oh, yes," Ham replied. Wallis perked up at the discussion of gift giving. *So, he is listening*, she thought.

"He gives out gold and silver, jewels, amulets, and goblets. Whatever we've won in battle, he shares with his men. We've both gotten something, haven't we, Wallis?"

Wallis simply looked at him, gave a low grunt, and went back to watching the rest of the camp pass by, though a slight tilt of his head proved he was still listening.

"You received a gift?" Judith asked.

"Of course," Ham replied. "I've received many gifts, though not as many as this old warrior," he said as he shrugged toward his companion. "Still, it's been a fair number. I could retire and live comfortably if I wanted to. But why would anyone want to do that? If I were to retire, what would I do all day? There is nothing else for me but fighting. Farm life isn't for me, and I don't know a single trade. Best I can hope for is to be an advisor to my lord, but that won't happen for a number of years. So, I fight. I have no patience for watching crops grow."

Judith carefully considered what the guard was saying. He didn't want to work hard in the fields, nor did he know a trade. He was too old to learn one anyway, which he didn't seem to mind. Ham seemed rather fond of his place in this world. *And why wouldn't he? Everything he needs is provided*, she noted.

"I'm sure tonight will be an absolutely wonderful time," Judith said. Then lost in her thoughts, she accidentally uttered, "I wish

I could attend, too."

Both guards laughed loudly at her suggestion.

"Not likely," Ham said as he and Wallis caught their breath. "Outsiders aren't allowed. Only the scop, but he's been with us so long we forget he didn't start the journey with us back in the north."

"Of course," Judith replied, "it was foolish of me to even mention it." She could feel the color rising in her cheeks. *Mind your tongue,* she reminded herself.

"Well, nobody is going to be around the camp tonight," Ham said. "If you'd like to, you can sneak closer and listen to the scop sing. He's magnificent."

"That would be lovely," Judith said, appreciative that Ham was trying to make her feel better. "I would love to hear his voice again." She was just beginning to fidget, not knowing what else she could ask questions about, when Nerienda rounded the corner.

The old maid looked at Wallis, who was clearly the more suspicious of the two men on watch. She smiled at him and said, "Thank you kindly. I feel much warmer now. A bit fatigued, though. I find I need to rest much sooner than the young ones. Funny how quickly it sneaks up on you, isn't it?"

Wallis smiled for the first time that day. He wasn't as old as Nerienda, but he certainly wasn't young anymore either.

"Aye," he agreed. "It happens fast. One minute you can go for days without sleep and the next you can't get through the day without two naps."

"Isn't that the truth?" Nerienda smiled. "Though I believe I'm now up to three."

Wallis laughed and held back the tent's entrance so Nerienda could go back inside and lie down.

Judith smiled. She had never seen Nerienda take a nap in her life. She turned once more to her new friend. "Thank you for answering my questions. I have just one more."

"Oh, what is that?" Ham asked.

She spoke sweetly and made a show of playing with the gold necklace she was wearing. "Tell me, what is Holofernes like at these feasts?"

Ham answered proudly. "He is the lord of lords. He eats more than the rest of us. He laughs louder, and he drinks twice as much as any man. He can hold his liquor well. Of course, at any feast, everyone gets drunk, but it does seem to take him longer. When he is drunk, though, he is generous. One time, he gave a man a gilded war axe just because he saw him chop off an enemy's arm with a single swing of his sword. It was quite a gift. We were all jealous that night."

"I can imagine," Judith said, though try as she might, she really couldn't. Picturing a man's arm fall to the ground after one hit with a sword seemed impossible. Instead of trying to take the details further, she merely said, "I'm glad he is kind."

"Oh, kind isn't the right word," Ham corrected. "Generous, benevolent, charismatic, all of those, but kind... our lord is not kind. Nor compassionate. He lacks both of those virtues."

"Well," Judith said, "I suppose that if a lord were to be lacking in virtues, those would be the two best ones."

"Agreed. And he is fair toward his men, unless his temper gets the better of him—as long as you do your job, it's unlikely you'll run into any trouble with him."

Judith smiled and got up to enter the tent. Just as she was about to take a step inside, she turned back and looked at the young guard once again.

"One more thing. I'm to see Holofernes tonight after the feast."

Wallis let out a grunt. It was clear he wanted no part in the conversation. Ham looked uncomfortable too, but Judith continued anyway. "I was just wondering if you knew what would please our lord tonight."

"Your hair is golden, yes?" Ham asked her, almost in a whisper.

Judith nodded. "Like yours."

He smiled. "Wear it in a long braid, no veil."

Judith blushed a little. Not wearing a veil was a sign of intimacy that only husbands and wives shared, and no man alive had ever seen her head uncovered as a grown woman.

The guard saw her discomfort, and he continued. "I didn't mean about camp, but simply when it's just the two of you... remove your veil and have your hair in a braid. Holofernes likes that best."

Despite her best judgment, Judith asked, "How do you know this?"

"We learn a lot about each other at our feasts. That's one thing we all know about Holofernes."

"Thank you," she whispered. Without further delay, she stepped back inside the safety and comfort of her small sanctuary.

CHAPTER 18

As Judith entered the tent, she nearly collided with Nerienda who was standing directly behind the entrance, listening to every word. She looked at Judith and nodded approvingly. "Good girl," she whispered. "Smart."

"Did you get it?" Judith whispered back.

Nerienda held up the plants and mushrooms, all nicely charred. She went to the small wooden stump they used as a chair, grabbed a rock from the ground, and began to smash the nightshade and mushrooms into a powder. It took a bit of time, but when she was done, she had a small, fine pile in front of her. Carefully, she scooped up what she could and put it into the vial.

Nerienda gave the small vial to Judith. "Slip it into his drink when he isn't looking. Make sure he has at least one good swallow. Once that's done, it's only a matter of minutes before he falls asleep. When he is asleep, his body will slowly shut down. By morning he will be dead, and we will be long gone."

Nodding, Judith asked one last question. "Where should I put the vial so it can't be found?"

Nerienda shot her a look that said, *Do I really have to answer that?* The sweet girl was so innocent she really had no idea.

"Hide it in your bosom. It will be safe, and no man would consider looking there. Not even Holofernes, at least at first, but you'd better take care of the poison quickly."

Nerienda could see the worry in the girl's eyes. She took both of her hands and said, "Judith, I am very proud of you. You have done so much in this short time, and you have shown how strong and courageous you truly are. When you left Bethulia just a few days ago, you were merely a girl praying for her people. Now you are as much a warrior as any noble thane, and you will be our city's savior."

Judith began to blush again and was about to disagree, but Nerienda continued. "I'm serious. You are a hero whether you want to be or not. It's time to stop doubting yourself. You must succeed. It's the only option for you, for me, and for everyone else we know."

"I'll try my best," Judith vowed. "And one more thing. If we can find that scop after the feast, we are taking him home with us."

***

The poison was ready. The escape route was planned. The sun was setting, and the feast was about to begin. Judith was finally about to stop and sit with her thoughts for the first time all day when Nerienda suddenly tore off her veil. Judith gasped in surprise. On instinct, her eyes darted around the room to make sure no man had seen it.

Nerienda barely gave the girl time to catch her breath before saying, "Hand me the comb from the bag."

Judith handed her the comb, and Nerienda brushed her hair over and over until it was as smooth and shiny as silk. Then she divided the blonde tresses into five sections. Judith's hair fell down to her waist, and with great skill Nerienda wove the golden hair and headband into the most intricate braid. It took a long while, but when she was done, the gold band once again sat on Judith's head like a delicate crown, and her long, gorgeous braid fell down her back.

Nerienda was lost in her task. When her mind wandered, it was only to pray that the girl would have the courage to kill Holofernes. *What a prayer!* she thought to herself. *Never in my wildest dreams would I have imagined I'd be uttering such a request.*

Meanwhile, Judith was lost in her own thoughts. Killing a man was not something she considered doing lightly, and she needed to be sure that murdering Holofernes was the only option to save her people. She carefully reviewed the events of the past few days. She remembered the wolf she'd killed and how scared she had been during her first meeting with Holofernes. She thought back to how he'd swept her off her feet that first night and how devastating it had been to find the doll in the treasure tent. After three days, she was finally able to see through Holofernes's façade.

He cannot love others, she thought to herself. *He only pretends to for his own gain. He is very convincing, I'll give him that, but his eyes have given away his true intentions more than once. He will continue to destroy everyone in his path until the day he dies. Dear Lord, please make that day be today.*

As Judith finished her prayer, Nerienda was finishing up the girl's hair. Then she carefully reapplied the last of the makeup they had with them. When she was done, the old woman was certain Holofernes would find the overall look pleasing.

Nerienda placed the veil over Judith's hair and gently secured it behind her neck. Then she reached into her pocket and took out the bird necklace. No damage had come to it, and she watched as the bird spun on its string, flying back and forth. Then she placed it securely around the girl's neck. With extra attention, she made sure to hide it under Judith's dress. No one would see it there, especially not with the necklace from Holofernes to distract them.

"Now, you are ready," she said.

Judith looked like the queen of a great lord, a confident woman who could achieve whatever she set out to do. The scared girl who left Bethulia had all but vanished.

Nerienda was making the final adjustments to the veil when Ham walked in on the women. Judith let out a small cry, and Nerienda quickly finished fastening her veil. When she was done, she turned around with a stern look. "What is the meaning of this?"

"A thousand apologies. I did not think I would interrupt you as I did. I only wanted to bring dinner quickly as the feast is about to start."

Keeping his gaze on the floor, the guard walked over to the stump in the corner and set down their food. Then he made a move to the door. He was just about to leave when he turned back to the women one last time.

"You'll be able to hear when the music begins. That's when everyone else gets quiet. Enjoy the music and enjoy your night with our lord. I'm sure your beauty will win him over tonight if it hasn't already."

"Thank you for everything," Nerienda said before Judith could reply. "We look forward to hearing the scop sing."

"Of course," Ham replied, happy to have helped. Then he departed with his head down and an embarrassed blush coloring his cheeks. The women could hear Ham and Wallis abandon their posts as they headed to the feast, and they found themselves completely alone for the first time since they had arrived at the camp.

CHAPTER 19

The moon rose on the horizon and the first stars began to appear just as the bonfires were being lit. A horn rang through the night—a call for the feast to commence. Rowe strummed a few cords on the harp for background music, and the feasting began.

The men celebrated like true Angles, eating their fill of roasted goat and lamb. They drank heavily, passing a golden goblet of mead from one man to the next, beginning with their lord, whom they all loved deeply in that moment. The men laughed and told stories and engaged in raucous, friendly fighting and one-upmanship. While the men ate and drank, Holofernes called on one or another, doting on him as he spoke of his courage, loyalty, and valiant deeds in battle.

There was Nodin, who had cut down twenty men with his broadsword and battle axe.

Upton was a legendary warrior who came from the east after he received an invitation to join Holofernes's infamous army and pledge his loyalty to the warlord. He was famous for singlehand-edly taking on a hippo in a far-off land. He'd forged into the water, jumped on the hippo's back, and thrust his spear into the behemoth's skull, right between the eyes. The animal gnashed its teeth, but Upton stayed clear of the powerful jaws, twisting his spear to be sure the damage done was lethal. As the animal sank under the water, Upton hopped off its back and made his way through the blood-red water. Because of his gallant behavior, the army was able to cross the river unharmed.

There was Wyman, who had been shot in the arm with an arrow as he dove in front of Holofernes. Had he not defended his lord, the arrow would have struck the commander in the heart and killed him. Wyman sacrificed his own body for his lord and then went on to kill three dozen enemy soldiers.

Holofernes praised these men and many others for their loyalty and bravery. Every story was met with applause and shouts of admiration from the men.

The revelry continued long into the night. There was cheering and singing, each man taking turns to share a story of their comrades' bravery. Every man also gave a toast to their lord, Holofernes, the greatest of ring bearers.

The food was abundant. Goats, sheep, and a few cattle, along with deer and wild boar were roasted and seasoned with the few spices the cooks had in the traveling pantry: salt, pepper, thyme, and sage. The meat was brought before the men on large platters, dripping with oily grease and fat. Onion and cabbage were served with the meat. Once a man had eaten his fill of one animal, he turned to another and began his ravished eating again.

The mead hall, where all feasts were held, was a place of happiness and gaiety. It was a place of security in a tumultuous world. The battlefield was dangerous, with only victory or death as the outcome; there was no such thing as retreat. The army relished in their many victories and brave accomplishments and anxiously awaited their dear lord to shower them with gifts. The din of the fellowship was carried on the wind until well after midnight, and if the Bethulians had been listening closely, they could have heard the jovial affair from within their own solemn walls.

***

Meanwhile, Judith and Nerienda sat in the entryway of their tent with the curtain pulled back. There was a soft, cool breeze blowing into their quarters as dusk passed and night settled in. They could hear the men's raucous laughter, the pounding of their feet, the thundering echoes as they banged their armor, and the all-around merriment of the moment.

They could even smell the food. The scent of the rich meats that had been roasting for days filled the tent whenever the cool air blew. Even the aroma of the sweet mead could be detected as they sat there watching the stars emerge in the sky one by one while they listened and waited.

Neither woman dared speak a word; Nerienda knew better than to interrupt Judith when she was thinking. The maiden was going through each step of their plan over and over again in her mind. The two women held hands, and Nerienda occasionally gave a soft squeeze to let Judith know she was still there.

The moon rose early at dusk and grew bright as it arched across the sky. Just as it was at its highest point, shining over the camp, the men finally quieted down. This was their cue. Judith and Nerienda stepped outside and made their way through the tents slowly and carefully. It was not hard now to figure out where they were going. The women had practically memorized the path to the center of the camp, and they knew the way out of the camp to Bethulia just as well, if not better.

After a short walk, the pair settled behind a tent a safe distance from the feast. There was still muffled talk but nothing that carried as far as the early conversations. It was only a few minutes after the women had settled that the young scop began to strum on his harp.

Rowe sang even more beautifully than he had earlier in the day, and his stories were all about the latest battle the army had won, as well as a few old favorites. The army listened to the scop's music with pride, but as Judith sat taking in the stories of battle, she thought of the fires she had seen in Bethulia the night Lord Godwine died. Holofernes's men had spent the last three years committing grave injustices; they had to be stopped.

The songs went on, and the stories of the battles filled Judith with courage and the confirmation that she was right in carrying out her plans. She was nervous but ready. She knew she had a great deal to accomplish. However, for the first time since Cyneric had brought the plan to her, Judith felt she might actually succeed.

She and Nerienda sat and listened as the boy peppered in the names of every thane and then spent a long time singing about Holofernes's bravery. The scop sang of their battles as if he had seen everything firsthand. He had a gift for turning the stories he'd heard around the campfires into a beautifully woven tapestry of melody and song.

He spoke about the men who had been lost. Only three this time. He gave them each a beautiful eulogy, emphasizing their loyalty and bravery. He noted they had preferred to die in battle at Holofernes's side than live anywhere else. The music and stories stretched long into the night, but no one seemed to mind. The smells of the food lingered in the air and mingled with Rowe's voice, creating a comfortable atmosphere that reminded everyone of home.

Even the women were touched by the beauty of the tunes. Judith knew many of the words to the songs were untrue, but the stories were so beautiful she didn't mind too much. Embellishments were a part of a scop's mead hall stories. The music was so moving she couldn't help but feel nostalgia for the days when her father was alive—the days when she felt like she truly belonged. Tears filled her eyes and escaped down her cheeks.

It was dark now in the camp, except for the glow of the bonfires where the men were gathered, and Judith allowed her mind to wander. It was only a week ago that she had been praying on her rooftop, asking the lord to bless her and her people, while hungry wolves surrounded the city waiting for the enemy to ravage them so they could feast beyond their wildest dreams. She had only prayed that deliverance would come. She never expected it would come by her hand. *If I am successful*, she thought.

She had been with the enemy for three days now. Her time with these men was coming to an end. By morning, if all went as planned, she would be home. However, home seemed very far away. *Do I have a home at all? A real home to call my own?* she wondered. *When I return to Bethulia, will everything be as it was? Will I still feel out of place?*

The last eulogy ended, the harp strings stopped, and the music slowly faded away. The night's gentle breeze carried the final note with it, sweeping it away toward the south. Judith didn't have time to answer her own questions before she was brought back to the present by shouts for another song. The crowd requested a popular bawdy drinking song well known by all. Rowe hesitated only a moment before strumming his harp again. In a matter of a few words, the men joined in, and they quickly drowned out the boy with their off-tune voices. Instead of a sweet harp, the women heard the men pounding their drinks on the table, singing along, and stomping their feet. The song was short, but when it ended, someone shouted for it to be repeated. So, the song was sung this way a dozen times before it finally came to an end. Once it had, all the men let out a great cheer.

In the middle of the raucous clamor, one voice came through more clearly than the rest. "To Holofernes, a lord among men! May he live long, eat well… and learn to be more generous with his spoils in war!" As soon as the words passed the drunk man's lips, the entire tent grew quiet.

"What did you say to me?" Holofernes roared.

There was a muffled pleading and loud apology. "I'm sorry, my lord. I meant nothing of it. It was a joke. Of course you are generous."

"Never say such things in the presence of your lord. Never say such things about me ever!"

The women looked at each other. They could tell the thane's words were meant as a joke, but they were the only two sober people in the camp.

"Toland," Holofernes continued, "this man seems to find me lacking generosity. An example needs to be made of him. Perhaps he will find me generous then. I've a mind to cut off his hand… never bite the hand that feeds you, and all that. But then he wouldn't make for a very good soldier, would he? And I am a generous lord after all."

"You are, sir," Toland said.

"Very well. In my generosity, you verbose buffoon, I will spare your hand."

"Thank you, my lord," the man shouted in relief.

"Toland, cut off his ear instead. It will heal much faster, and he only needs one to hear anyway."

Without further instruction, Toland drew his dagger, walked over to the thane, and pulled his ear taut with one hand. "We'll do this on the out breath," he whispered. The thane gave a nearly imperceptible nod. He inhaled… and then Toland sliced his ear off in one swift motion.

The scream was primal—high-pitched and guttural all at once. Judith's eyes filled with tears. She couldn't breathe, and her hands began to shake. Nerienda grabbed Judith's hand in her own.

"Breathe," she commanded, as much to herself as to Judith. For a few moments, they sat trembling with tear-soaked faces. When they were finally able to calm themselves, Judith gave Nerienda's hand a squeeze.

"Are you certain we are up for this task?" she asked.

Nerienda took a deep breath. "You're poisoning him, not chopping off his ear. It should be much quieter. And, if nothing else, we've at least heard what we're up against. It won't be so startling next time."

Judith's eyes grew wide. Her heart was racing, but she tried to put on a brave face as she forced herself to take slow, deep breaths. She turned her attention back to the feast, but she couldn't hear what was happening next. She assumed it was time for the gifts to be given out.

Nerienda pulled on Judith's hand. "If they see us here, we will be in trouble. We must go back to the tent now."

They quickly returned to their tent, crept inside, and closed the entrance firmly behind them.

Nerienda lit their single small candle, and the two women relaxed in the safe, familiar surroundings. Their shadows started to dance across the animal skins, leaving them in the familiar glow, cut off from the outside world one last time. Having been up so late,

Nerienda began to doze off, but Judith was far too awake to rest. Instead of sleeping, she sat and prayed. There was no roof to climb onto tonight, but the coziness of the tent managed to bring her the same familiar comfort.

For months she had asked God to send Bethulia a miracle. She had hoped that something great would happen so that her people would be saved. As it turned out, the opportunity for something great had presented itself, though not the way she had planned. She thought about the blacksmith who had helped her. She thought about the farmers who had spent months smuggling their crops through the secret opening in the city wall without the townspeople ever knowing of their bravery. She thought about Olaf, the wild man who escorted them to the camp. And she thought about her friends and neighbors—especially Ellette. *The horrors that will happen to them if I fail!* She shuddered in fear.

She could see clearly now. Holofernes destroyed towns, cities, and families. Worse still, he butchered children. She picked up the doll that was hidden in the corner. She held it close for a while, hoping the embrace would comfort her. She prayed that the child who had once owned it was resting in peace. Then, once again, she prayed for strength. She begged that the burning desire in her heart for justice and salvation would not waver.

Dear Lord, help me carry out this mighty feat—this call for vengeance burning so deeply in my heart. I know I am no match for the monster I have been sent to kill, but with your help, all things are possible. Give me strength, Lord, to fight as bravely as any thane. And please, no matter what happens to me tonight, save Bethulia.

CHAPTER 20

Judith heard footsteps coming. She had just enough time to shove the doll into the food bag before a man entered.

"Let's go," he ordered.

Judith didn't recognize the deep voice and couldn't quite make out the man's face in the shadows, but she dutifully walked out of the tent. As she stepped out, she immediately recognized the silhouette in front of her. It was Knut. She hadn't recognized the voice because she had never heard the man speak.

Judith expected Knut to grab her wrist and drag her through the camp, but he seemed different. Instead of the rigid, imposing stance she was accustomed to, Judith could just make out a slight wobble. Slowly, he swayed back and forth. In the bright moonlight she could make out the shape of his mouth and the firmness of his jaw.

Knut stared down at her, studying her features. Despite the fog that clouded his vision, he could see Judith in all her radiance. He was just like any other man in the camp. Though he was gruff and silent, Judith's beauty affected him as much as it did everyone else. *How easy would it be to take her for myself before I presented her to Lord Holofernes?* he thought. But even in a drunken stupor, the fear of his lord caused him to hesitate.

Holofernes had a habit of falling asleep quickly after a feast—a sleep so deep it was impossible to wake him. Knut doubted Judith's presence in his tent would be missed. Still, he knew the rules… and yet, Judith's beauty made it hard for him to follow orders.

After a long moment, he noticed a strange look on her face. Something seemed off. Was she just scared of him, or was she hiding something? He grabbed Judith by the arm and felt along the bodice and the folds of her dress to see if there was anything unusual hidden in them. When he found nothing there, he lifted the folds of Judith's skirt and began to feel his way up her bare legs, stopping at the highest point of the upper thigh.

Judith shivered with fear. She thought Knut would continue up her hips, but he suddenly stopped and tore open the bodice of her dress instead. Judith wanted to scream, but she stood still, praying the assault would end quickly. Knut felt her breasts under the thin layer of coarse linen, and as his thumbs closed in around them, he found the small vial. He grabbed it from Judith's bosom and held it to the moonlight.

"What is this?" he barked.

Paralyzed with fear, Judith was unable to answer.

When Knut refused to break his stare, Judith finally whispered, "Nothing, just perfume."

Knut opened the vial and inhaled deeply. "It smells like shit," he stammered and threw the vial on the ground, crushing it with the heel of his boot. "That wasn't perfume, was it?"

"It was. I swear," Judith replied, frightened for her life.

Knut became enraged. He balled her veil up in his fist and yanked it off, exposing her braided hair. Judith had never felt so naked and vulnerable in her life. However, she dared not attempt to cover herself, knowing full well that any sign of weakness could lead to dangerous consequences.

The sight of Judith's golden hair enflamed Knut's passion. He grabbed her wrist and dragged her toward an empty tent only a few yards away, but Judith dug her feet into the ground and resisted with all her might.

She opened her mouth to cry out, but he clamped his hand over it. He leaned in and whispered, "If you so much as make a squeak, I will kill you and your maid both."

Judith stopped resisting. Knut tightened his grip, took a step forward, and pulled Judith against him. He unbuckled his pants and thrust his pelvis against her hips. Then he bent down to bring his face inches from hers. His strong breath filled Judith's nostrils, and the smell made her feel ill.

Knut had a fiery look in his eye, one of passion mixed with something much deeper—violence. Judith tried to lean away from him, but he grabbed the back of her head and brought her closer. She cringed as she prepared for the worst.

Just as Knut was about to kiss her, his grip on the back of her head relaxed and his wild eyes bulged. His tongue went limp and fell onto his bottom lip as he let out a soft groan. He stood where he was for a long moment before crumbling to his knees. Nerienda stood behind the dying thane with the blacksmith's blade bloody and glistening in the moonlight.

Nerienda wiped her hands on her dress and used the bottom of her veil to clean her face. Then she wiped the blade off on the inside of her cloak before turning her attention to Judith. The girl seemed unharmed. Even her dress had not been torn too much—at least not in a way that one could notice unless he looked closely.

"Quickly now," Nerienda rushed over and gave the girl a warm hug. She picked Judith's veil up off the ground, shook it out, and secured it in place after making sure her braid was still intact and headband secure. Then she fixed up Judith's bodice as best she could and smoothed out the folds of her skirts. Once she was done, the girl looked as radiant as she had only moments earlier, despite the lack of color in her face and the slight tremble of her hands.

Judith stood motionless, struggling to comprehend what had just happened. She had felt brave as she sat in the tent, but after such a confrontation, she was more scared now than ever. Nerienda gave her a sharp but firm pat on the cheek.

"Come back to me, Judith. Now is not the time to break. We have just killed one of Holofernes's closest thanes. There is no turning back now."

Judith pulled herself together. The women looked around, making sure no one was nearby. Voices spoke in the distance, but those speaking were too drunk to comprehend. Most of the men were already asleep. Their snores carried out from the tents to where the women stood.

Looking down at Knut, they puzzled over what to do with the body. Finally, Nerienda spoke.

"We are going to put him in our tent and close the entrance as if I was still asleep inside. We'll snuff out the candle, and I'll take our bag with us. Then we are going to Holofernes's tent on our own. We can't let anyone see us. Once there, sneak inside and wait for him. If he is already there, pretend Knut has just brought you to him. I will hide just outside the tent, and I will watch and listen to make sure the path is clear for our departure."

Judith looked at the blade Nerienda was still holding. Nerienda followed her eyes and continued, "I will keep this in case I need it again."

"But how am I supposed to kill Holofernes? The poison is gone."

"You will find your way—one God will provide for you. You must. Use a blanket, a razor, your bare hands. Whatever you can find. It must be done."

Judith nodded and picked up Knut's feet as Nerienda grabbed his arms. They painstakingly dragged him through the dirt into the tent as far as they could. The man was twice their size and nearly three times their weight. He was the biggest man in Holofernes's army, and he would surely be missed in the quickly approaching morning. They had no choice but to complete their mission tonight.

When they went back outside to see if they had left anything, they found a trail of blood that led right into their tent. Nerienda kicked as much dirt over it as she could in an attempt to make it look like spilled mead. Then they went inside and gathered their things. Nerienda grabbed the bag with their few possessions, and Judith threw her cloak on over her torn dress, hoping it would hide the hastily patched bodice.

Before they left, the women said a final prayer for strength and wisdom. Their plans were ruined, and they were left to rely on faith and instinct.

Nerienda walked over to the candle and blew it out. Then, trying not to trip over the giant lying on the ground, the two women made their way to the entrance. Just before they walked out into the night, Nerienda grabbed Judith by the arm.

"After you have succeeded," she whispered, "remember to take some sort of token so that we can prove you have killed him. We will need something to show that Holofernes is dead."

Judith nodded, and the two women walked toward Holofernes's tent. Nerienda took no chances, arming herself with the dagger low at her side, halfway hidden by the folds of her cloak. Luckily, there were just a few soldiers wandering around drunk, and the women were able to bypass them quickly. Once they approached the center of camp, they saw a small group of men wrestling and laughing. The large bonfires from the feast were still a fair distance, so Judith and Nerienda thought the light was dim enough for them to pass unseen if they stayed in the shadows. However, in their haste, they walked in front of a torchlight. One of the men caught a glimpse of their movement.

"Who's there?" he yelled as everyone else stopped to peer into the darkness.

No one responded, so the thane went to investigate.

The women hid behind a tent, but they could feel the man approaching. They stood in the shadows, holding their breath, while Nerienda clutched the blade in her hand and Judith said a silent prayer.

As the soldier rounded the corner, they saw it was Acwel. Though he was drunk, his mind was still sharp.

"What are you doing?" he asked in a near whisper as his eyes fell on Nerienda's dagger.

"We are on our way to Holofernes," Judith said.

"Where's Knut? He was supposed to go get you."

Judith paused for a moment too long, and Acwel caught her hesitation.

"He was too drunk to take us. He was practically falling over when he arrived. We encouraged him to rest in our tent," Judith blurted out.

Acwel's eyes narrowed. "If that's so, then perhaps I should go check on him."

"No. Please…" Judith said. She took off her gold bracelets and gave them to Acwel. "Here. Take these for your trouble. Please return to your friends."

At once, the pieces fit together in Acwel's mind. He thought back to their story on the first day. *A noblewoman and her maid could never spend days running through a forest. Nor would they be armed.*

As Acwel studied them closely, he spotted the bloodstain on Nerienda's sleeve that they had forgotten to hide. Judith was very good at lying, he gave her that, but he had caught them. Now, it was up to him to decide their fate. However, he could see that his actions in this moment could change his fate too. He was tired of fighting. This crusade was far longer than he had originally signed up for, and his conscience afforded him little rest. He had saved the scop years ago in the hopes that it would ease his guilt, but it hadn't. It couldn't. One life saved, while he took hundreds by his own hand. It wasn't enough. For months, all he had wanted was to return to his family. Now, he was being offered the means to get there with some beautiful bracelets. He stepped forward and took them from Judith. Carefully, he opened the pouch he always carried on his belt and let the contents fall into his hand. Judith noticed the few gold pieces, several silver, and half a dozen precious stones... some emeralds, sapphires, one ruby, and one small garnet—so dark it looked almost black.

"I know what you're doing," he whispered as he added the bracelets to his small hoard and returned it all. "This is a dangerous game you're playing. You cannot lose."

"You're not going to stop us?" Judith asked, eyes wide.

"No. Holofernes has killed too many innocent people. And it's time for me to go home. I miss my wife, and my son is nearly a man now."

"How can we trust you?" Nerienda demanded.

"You can't. You can't trust any of us. We sold our souls for a chance at riches and greatness when we joined Holofernes's army.

But he has brought us neither, just infamy and more fighting. The gifts he gives are only one tenth of what we take from the towns. He keeps the rest for himself... unless you have quick hands." Acwel gave a sly smile. "You'll just have to take me at my word. But if you give me your rings, I'll be sure not to warn the others."

Judith quickly took them off and handed them over as well.

"I sold my soul, but hopefully these will help me buy it back. One last thing... make up a better story about Knut. No one will believe he was too drunk to stand."

Judith nodded, and Acwel returned to the group of men still wrestling as Judith and Nerienda hurried to Holofernes's tent.

"It was just Bart," Acwel yelled to the men loud enough for the women to hear. "Remember he went to get more mead? Stupid drunkard got lost on the way to his own tent."

Raucous laughter followed as the men went back to their games. The women breathed a small sigh of relief and carried on, staying in the shadows, weaving around the mostly abandoned tents until they came within a few paces of Holofernes's quarters. Nerienda settled herself safely behind a dark corner of a tent that proved an excellent hiding spot.

"I will be right here," she said. "If anyone stops you, tell them Knut had to leave you because he heard a wolf and that you are to see Holofernes immediately. Be sure your necklace is prominent. This close to the lord's tent, no one will touch you. Be brave. The more confident you are, the less likely they'll be suspicious."

Judith gave Nerienda one last hug. Then, drawing all of her strength, she threw back her shoulders, carefully smoothed the folds of her cloak and dress, and stepped out from the shadows into the firelight.

CHAPTER 21

As Judith walked toward the center of camp, a sense of calm washed over her. She wasn't sure what she would find in Holofernes's tent, but she had a sudden inner peace that assured her everything would work out. Carefully, she stepped forward with her arms at her side and her head held high. She looked around as she went and noticed that the group of wrestlers was far away now. She could also see inside the tent used for the feast; many of the thanes lay fast asleep at the table. The few men walking around had their arms around each other as they stumbled back to their tents.

She was halfway to Holofernes's tent, trying not to draw attention to herself, when Toland appeared out of nowhere. Though he could stand on his own, the smile on his flushed face told her he had been drinking a fair amount too. He came up to Judith and asked with slurred speech, "Why are you here? What are you doing?"

Judith noticed he was clutching a gold helmet. "I'm here to see Holofernes," she answered calmly.

As if it sparked a memory, Toland held up a finger. "Ah, yes. That's right. We sent Knut for you. Where is he?"

For half a second Judith froze, but then remembered that nobody had seen what had happened.

"He was escorting me here when a wolf emerged from the forest and started growling at us," she replied. "He told me to go on ahead, and he would follow when he was done. When I left, he had the wolf's head in the crook of his arm and held his knife just over the beast's heart. I didn't wait to see the rest."

"Leave it to Knut to wrestle a wild beast after a feast. While the rest of the men sleep, he's the one who's out fighting. A born killer he is." Toland let out a long, hard laugh at the thought of his friend wrestling the wolf in his drunken state. Then he looked at Judith again as if noticing her for the first time. He eyed her up and down then walked around her in a circle.

"Very well," he finally sighed with fatigue. "Holofernes is not here yet. He is still at the feast, but he should be coming shortly. Wait inside his tent for him. Do you need anything to eat or drink?"

Judith smiled at him before answering. "Actually, a small cup of mead would be appreciated."

Toland smiled broadly. Clearly, he was much happier when he was drunk. He shouted to someone across the way, ordering the drink be brought over. The man did his best to hurry, but he couldn't quite walk in a straight line. Toland doubled over with laughter, and Judith felt it was best to humor the two men and laugh as well.

Once the drink arrived, Toland held back the entrance to the tent and, with an air of whimsy, gave a low bow as he ushered her in.

"Make yourself comfortable. If you need anything, I will be right out here."

Judith thanked him sweetly, but as she entered the tent, she grew worried. If Toland was going to be waiting outside, how was she going to escape when the time came? And what if he heard what was happening in the tent?

Just when she was at the point of panicking, the sense of calm and peace returned. Even if she didn't get out alive, she would make sure that Holofernes didn't make it either. Cyneric's words echoed in her mind. *Carry out your plan by any means necessary.* There was already more blood on Judith's and Nerienda's hands than she wanted, but the death of two more evil men seemed a small price to pay if it meant saving her city.

When she stepped into Holofernes's tent, Judith was taken aback by how beautiful and elaborate the room was. It was well lit with many candles, and the gold and silver ornaments decorating the quarters glistened in the light. There was a large bed in the center of the room—comfortable and big enough for two men the size of Holofernes. It was covered in rich blankets and soft pillows. At one end of the tent sat a small, ornately crafted table. Approaching the table, she noticed that all the maps Holofernes had been looking at the first morning were neatly folded and piled on top with markings here and there.

There was a side table that held a pitcher and a bowl for washing. Holofernes even had a small mirror in the tent, a sign of affluence amongst travelers. *And perhaps a bit of vanity*, she smiled to herself. Judith dropped her wool cloak on a cushion she spied in another corner. As she turned around, something at the head of the bed caught her eye. It was a canopy that encircled the bed when it was fully opened. She pulled it out and examined it. The delicate fabric seemed to be completely opaque when she tried to look at it from the outside. She pulled it out an arm's length and the room lit up with a beautiful golden glow as the curtain reflected the candlelight. Though it was lightweight, the cloth seemed to be impenetrable. *Just another form of security while Holofernes sleeps.*

She pulled the curtain halfway around the bed and sat down. The bed was even softer than it looked, and the mattress was filled with feathers. Judith was so enthralled by the luxury surrounding her that it took her a while to look up at the curtain again. When she finally did, she gasped. Even though it was impossible to see the bed when the curtain was around it, it was easy to see out. She could see everything! This was a curtain unlike any she had seen before, a beautiful protection for the person who slept inside. *Fascinating!* She moved the curtain back to where she had found it and stood.

Still unsure of what to do with herself, she went over to the washbasin, washed her hands in the cool water, and splashed the back of her neck to calm herself. When she was done, she began looking for a weapon. She rummaged through the drawers and trunks, trying to find something, anything that would do. Finally, as she was looking through the maps on the table, she found something that could possibly work. It was a small, sharp file.

I wonder what this is for? Perhaps he uses it in the mornings when he is working, she thought. She could vaguely remember Toland holding it when she first met him. She picked it up and tucked it under her sleeve. It was so thin and small she could barely feel it. But if she had to, she could drive it deep into Holofernes's heart. It wouldn't be as clean or as quiet as poison, but she didn't have much choice.

Judith sat down on the bed again, this time facing the doorway. Remembering Ham's words, she removed her veil and patted the top of her head to make sure her headband was still in place. To be sure Holofernes could see her long braid, she pulled it over her shoulder. In the light of the candles, her beautiful blonde hair glowed with a golden warmth. She was unsure whether she should do anything else, but she didn't have much time to think, as she heard footsteps approaching. She took a few deep breaths as she listened to the lord speak with Toland. Their conversation was slightly muffled, but she could make out enough of it to understand what was going on.

"A good night for a feast," Holofernes began jovially.

Toland answered with just as much enthusiasm. "And what a feast! Absolutely the best we could have, my lord."

"I should hope so. We've gone to great lengths to make sure there was none greater, and every man who had a part played it well."

"That they did. My lord..." There was a moment of silence before Toland continued. "Judith is waiting for you inside your tent."

Holofernes replied a little too loudly. "Fantastic! A wonderful ending to a wonderful night."

"And she looks radiant," Toland continued.

"Oh," Holofernes joked, "have you looked closely?"

Toland laughed, unafraid of the veiled threat. "Not at all, my lord, but her radiance cannot be overlooked tonight."

"Good, I'm glad she is taking my proposal seriously. If she wants to be my queen, she had better know how to please me."

Judith stiffened at his words, but she did her best to relax, knowing that her nerves could give her away.

"You look a bit tired, my lord. Are you sure you don't want me to send the girl away and have her come back tomorrow instead?"

No! That can't happen, Judith thought. *Tonight is the only night we have.*

Fortunately, Holofernes was of a similar mind—although for very different reasons. "Of course not," he said. "She is to be my queen, and were there a priest in the area, she would be already."

Judith realized at this moment that Toland, whether he knew it or not, was the only person who could stop her from what she was about to do. He had Holofernes's best interests in mind no matter where he was or what state he was in.

Holofernes smiled again. "Do you doubt my stamina, Toland?"

"Of course not, my lord. You once fought for three days in the rain and mud and killed nearly half the enemy army yourself! I know your stamina!" The two men laughed loudly.

"Then don't doubt me. Tonight will be far more comfortable than fighting in the rain and mud, and though I could go on, I certainly won't take three days."

Judith was growing very uncomfortable with the conversation. Holofernes and Toland were now so loud she worried they would wake the entire army. Furthermore, she did not want her mission to take any longer or become any more complicated than it had to be. Dawn was coming. Escape would be much harder without the darkness to conceal them. Judith shuddered to think what might happen if she and Nerienda were not back in Bethulia by the time the sun came up.

As she stood waiting, her patience grew thin and doubt crept in. She felt, once again, incapable of the task she was about to perform. *What if I'm not strong enough physically? But Nerienda killed Knut by herself. Surely, I can do it too.* She was soothed for only a moment before an even more worrisome idea came to her. *What if his charm and charisma is so strong tonight that I can't resist him?*

Judith took a deep breath and straightened up. She tried to push her doubts from her mind and said a quick but fervent prayer. "Lord, please come to my aid in my hour of need. I know you have called me to complete this task for my people, but I feel weak and unfit. Lord, please give me the courage and grace to complete Your will. Have mercy on me for what I am about to do, and soothe the fires of my soul so that I may carry out your will in faith and trust in You. Amen."

Just as she was finishing up, Holofernes and Toland ended their conversation too.

"Thank you again, my lord, for the beautiful gift you have given me. I will treasure the helmet forever. It is indeed a masterpiece. Whoever the craftsman was deserves much praise, though I suppose he is no longer around to hear it."

"You suppose? You sliced off his head with his own sword." They laughed again.

"Good night, Toland," Holofernes said. "I will see you in the morning. Don't bother to wait up. You know I'm safe. And try to ignore anything you might hear."

"Oh, my lord, you are too much sometimes," Toland said through a smile. With a final roar of laughter, the two men embraced each other, slapping one another's backs.

Judith drew herself up to her highest height and let out a slow breath. Her heart steadied. Her anxiety vanished, and her mind cleared. She felt ready for whatever was about to come; almost as if a higher power had taken hold of her. She smiled pleasantly, hoping the expression revealed the excitement she was supposed to be feeling, and she watched with curiosity as Holofernes, still laughing, pulled back the entrance to his tent and stepped inside.

CHAPTER 22

Holofernes found Judith standing in front of his bed with a regal air about her. Her dress was beautiful, her face was radiant as ever, and an alluring braid offset by a delicate headdress of gold cascaded over her shoulder. Holofernes knew Judith had blonde hair but was amazed at how golden it actually was. In the flickering candlelight, she looked like an ethereal beauty.

She must be a fairy, he thought. He was almost afraid to step closer, worried that this vision might vanish.

Sensing his hesitation, Judith decided to make the first move and gave a small bow. Then she took one small step forward and said, "My lord, it is good to see you tonight."

Holofernes loved Judith's boldness as much as he loved her beauty. He loved her strength, wisdom, and innocence. He had known her less than three days, but he'd already decided she was the only woman in the country fit to be his queen. Now, seeing her bow, he started to relax. It was clear she wasn't going to float away, and his irrational fears evaporated. Still, he didn't respond but only continued to stare at her.

Unsure how to proceed, he himself gave a bow. He knew how to fight in battle and lead his men—those were things he had been doing nearly all his life. What he knew so little about was how to act around women he respected. He finally tried to move toward Judith, but the mead was catching up to him and the room began to spin. He grasped the corner of the ornate desk just in time to keep himself from falling.

"My lord," Judith said, running to him, "are you alright? Is there anything I can do to help you?"

Embarrassed that he looked weak, Holofernes quickly steadied himself. Judith saw her mistake. She had made him feel weak. *Make him think he is still in control.* Her eyes caught his reflection in the mirror. *Compliment him.* Holofernes was still dressed in his finest armor. He looked as a lord, as a true leader should.

"My lord," she said, "you look like a warrior tonight. Dressed more richly than any lord I have ever encountered." Taking a small step forward, she quieted her voice, "And you are very handsome."

At this, Holofernes stopped and stood up straight. He stared into Judith's eyes and refused to look away. He carefully removed his crown and began to unfasten the armor covering his chest and back. It was a slow process, and he took his time. Still staring at Judith, his passion for her increased by the second. All his charm had vanished, and in its place was a primal lust.

He smells of stale mead and sweat, Judith thought, disgusted, but she met his gaze and tried to look innocent and sweet. Holofernes clearly approved of what he saw, and she wasn't about to break eye contact. She watched him undress and remove his armor, his crown, and the many rings and bracelets adorning each hand. At long last, he stepped toward her, and Judith saw the sway in his gait.

The passion in his eyes became visible as he moved closer to Judith. His stare looked much like Knut's, only cloudier. His eyes darted back and forth like a rabid animal, unable to focus on anything for longer than a fleeting moment.

Holofernes neared the bed and reached down to unbuckle his belt. He placed his sword, still in its rusty sheath, above his bed just as he had said he did every night. Then he threw his belt on the floor and sat down to take off his shoes, but as he bent forward, he again felt the room spinning and lost focus.

Judith knelt down. "My lord, please allow me," she offered sweetly.

Holofernes let out a soft grunt, but he let Judith continue.

When his boots were removed, Judith stood up. She could see everything that Holofernes was trying to hide. She could see him swoon and sway and became slightly worried he might be ill. Even so, she thought things could be easier if he had just one more drink. As innocently as ever, she gave Holofernes's hand a gentle squeeze and went to retrieve her mead cup.

"Here, my lord," she said. "You look a little unwell. Perhaps you should have something to drink. Toland brought this for me, but I have had enough. Please, drink the rest."

With his mind clouded, Holofernes obediently took the cup and drained the rest. The last few drops seemed to push him over the edge. When he was done, he threw the cup onto the ground, grabbed Judith by the wrist and pulled her to him.

The beastly man tried to pull her into his lap, but his coordination was lacking. He quickly became frustrated. Despite his clumsiness, his strength remained. To please him, Judith quickly adjusted herself into the position she assumed he wanted. Her mind reeled as she tried to piece together an appropriate attack, but just as she started to panic, she noticed the lord was ready to pass out at any moment, he just needed a bit of a push in the right direction.

Wait till he is asleep, her thoughts whispered.

"You must be tired after such a long day, my lord. There is a song my people sing once night has fallen and it is time to sleep. Would you like to hear it?"

Holofernes only let out a low grunt, but Judith, pretending he responded coherently, smiled and began. It was a soft, slow lullaby that the women of Bethulia sang to their children before bed, one that Nerienda had sung to her many times. Judith carried the tune beautifully. She gently stroked Holofernes's greasy, wet face to draw him into deeper relaxation. As the last notes of the song ended, she reached up, put her hands on his shoulders, and gave him a gentle nudge. Holofernes's body tipped slowly onto the soft bed. His eyes rolled back into his head. He was passed out, drunk.

Waiting to be sure Holofernes was in a deep sleep, Judith stood over him for a long while. Then she tried shaking him, nudged his leg with her hand, and even hit him softly on the face a few times to see if he would stir, but the great man just lay there limp, unable to respond to anything. She could have been standing completely naked in front of him, and he wouldn't have known.

She stopped for a moment and listened to the sounds of the night. She could hear Toland snoring outside the tent. It was the deep snore of inebriation. Soon, Holofernes began to join in as well. His snore was more of a roar, thundering from the bellows of his gut.

Judith looked him over and was surprised by what she saw. So often when someone sleeps, they have a certain peace about them. Even the worst men can assume a soft kindness on their countenance as they dream. However, that was not the case with Holofernes. Judith thought he looked like an animal, cruel and wild. His true intentions were clearly written across his face. He was a man whose love was buried under his own selfishness and thirst for power. His expression reflected only violence and evil.

"Heathen dog," Judith murmured.

As she stood before him, contemplating what she was about to do, her mind started racing again. She remembered how Holofernes had spoken so sweetly to her in the last three days and how he had given her the beautiful necklace. He promised her his protection and then the world. She also thought about everything she had witnessed: his men who followed him so blindly and bravely, his quick temper and bouts of anger, all the jewels the army had stolen, the mead they had taken from pillaged towns. She thought of the small keepsakes—the pots and jewelry, even the necklace she wore, that had once belonged to someone else far away. Finally, she thought about the doll.

Fury burned within her. She reached for the file in her sleeve, but as she stood over Holofernes's girth, she knew such a small instrument would do little harm to him. He was simply too big and strong.

Judith was about to panic when something shimmered out of the corner of her eye. She looked up and realized it was the sheath of Holofernes's sword bouncing the candlelight around the tent. It was rusty and old, but the sword inside was sharp. She carefully lifted the weapon from its place above his bed and removed the sword, but it was heavier than she expected and fell to the ground in front of her. Even through her anger she was impressed that Holofernes had the strength to carry the sword at his belt so effortlessly day in and day out.

She took a deep breath. Looking over Holofernes one more time, she whispered, "You deserve to die in your sleep. Having the satisfaction of being awake and seeing your enemy is not a privilege afforded to you."

Then she stepped forward to adjust his head, making sure his neck was exposed. She picked up the sword and made a quick sign of the cross. She heaved the weapon up over her head. Her arms trembled from the heaviness of it, but she held it up for only a moment. Then she let the weight of the blade fall on Holofernes's bare neck.

The sword sunk deep into his flesh. Blood sprayed Judith's face, hair, hands, and dress. She was disgusted. She wanted to run, but as she looked up, she saw Holofernes's eyes open. They looked at her in one wild moment of recognition before rolling back into his head. *Can he still be alive?* she wondered. *Maybe one strike wasn't enough.*

Using all her might, she wedged the sword out of the deep wound. The blade dripped with blood. A crimson stream poured from Holofernes's neck, down his body, and onto the bedsheets and blankets. She lifted the weapon once more and let it fall onto Holofernes's neck in the exact same spot.

This time she heard the crunch of bones as the head was severed from the body. It rolled from the bed onto the floor and came to a stop at Judith's feet, the eyes open and tongue protruding.

It took a moment for Judith to register what she had just done. She stared for a long while at the limp, lifeless body, but when she finally understood that Holofernes was indeed dead, she dropped the sword to the ground and cried as the shock and fear of the past few moments caught up with her.

She had done it. No matter what happened next, she had done what she promised to do. With relief, she knelt down in the middle of the bloody scene and said a brief prayer of thanksgiving. Her eyes downcast in prayer, she noticed that the head had formed a pool of blood where she knelt. Her beautiful slippers were ruined, as was her dress.

She prayed so intently that she didn't even notice that Toland's snores had stopped. He coughed heavily and let out a low groan as he stretched. Judith sat up with a start. *How is he awake? I thought he was as drunk as the rest of them. Oh God, help me.*

Panic filled her chest as she scanned the room quickly. She needed to hide until she was certain Toland was either gone or asleep again. But the small tent had no corner to hide in. There was a rug off to one side. She bolted, grabbed the rug, and threw it over the blood-soaked ground. Then she put the head on the pillow it had rested on just moments before, threw all the blankets over the body, and drew the sheer gold curtain around them. She lay down next to Holofernes and covered herself with one of the blankets. The smell of blood was overpowering, but she hoped anyone looking in on them would be too drunk to notice.

She heard footsteps approaching and sucked in her breath.

"My lord," she heard Toland shout from the other side of the tent entrance. "How goes your evening?" Judith didn't even dare breathe.

"My lord?" Toland shouted louder and this time pulled back the entrance to peer inside.

The room was dark; a single candle flame burned on the small table. Judith wanted to scream. She covered her mouth with her hand to stifle the urge. Toland looked around the room. She could see him clearly through the curtain, but he struggled to make sense of the shadows and darkness before him.

"My lord?" Toland whispered once more. He strained to peer into the darkness and scanned the room that was so familiar to him. Everything looked in order. *But what is that? The rug is out of place. Is something under it?* He couldn't quite tell. He took a step forward when he noticed Judith's cloak thrown over the chair.

"Ah, yes. He has a guest tonight. Must have worn himself out." He chuckled. He made to go back to his post when he got a whiff of a foul smell. "Holofernes, are you alright?" he called louder this time.

Judith watched Toland like a hawk. She felt something wet on her neck. Holofernes's blood was dripping from his head and the smell was getting stronger by the moment. Thinking fast, Judith let out a deep, low moan followed by a breathy, sensuous cry.

Immediately, Toland dropped his gaze down to the ground. "My apologies, my lord," he said as he made a hasty retreat.

Judith breathed a sigh of relief the moment he was out of sight, but she didn't dare move until she heard Toland's snores once again.

Judith lifted the severed head by its hair and peered into its eyes. She had considered taking Holofernes's sword with her as a sign she had killed him, but it was far too heavy to carry all the way back to Bethulia. As she watched the blood drain out of his head and onto her skirt, she decided then and there to take it back instead. Not only would it be a sure sign of her victory, but it would also serve as one final insult to an army that thought itself invincible.

The room was as bloody a massacre as any on the open battlefield, even goats and sheep were killed more humanely, but Judith was too stunned to care about cleaning up. She had done her job and now it was time to leave. Before she could, though, she remembered to retrieve her veil. She found it at Holofernes's feet. It had been spared most of the blood spatter, though there were still a few flecks on the back of it. Quickly, she picked it up and tucked it under her arm. Then she ripped the gold necklace off her neck, dropped it on the ground, and turned to leave.

Toland was still snoring loudly, but she could hear nothing else. When she carefully peeked her head outside, there was no one around. The firelight was all but gone. Only hot coals remained, smoldering with a soft orange glow. The men nearby were passed out snoring.

Judith stepped out into the night and made her way past Toland

and the other sleeping men clutching Holofernes's head in one hand and her veil in the other. Not one man stirred as she walked by. She was trembling, but she took in large gulps of the fresh night air, happy to be away from the stifling stench of blood and death.

CHAPTER 23

Nerienda heard footsteps coming but was unsure who they belonged to. She had not met any thanes yet, but she was afraid her luck was running out. The old woman was growing worried. She clenched the blacksmith's dagger, ready to attack.

After Judith left her alone, the minutes had passed slowly, and Nerienda prayed for the girl. She had hoped the whole messy ordeal could be carried out in the span of just a few moments, and though she knew it would be impossible to kill a man so quickly, she had not anticipated the wait to be quite this long. At first, she petitioned God to give Judith strength and courage. However, it did not take long before Nerienda found herself simply begging for the girl to return to her. She did not even care whether Holofernes lived or died, she only wanted to return to the safety of their walled city with Judith.

Nerienda panicked as the steps grew closer. When she recognized Judith's silhouette, relief swept over her, and she hugged the girl close. As she stepped back, she noticed the object at Judith's side. She let out a gasp so loud that both women looked around to be sure they hadn't been heard.

"Gracious, Judith," Nerienda hissed. "I said a token, not his whole head."

Before Judith could answer, Acwel stepped out of the shadows. The women froze as he approached. When he was just a few paces away, he stopped and looked down for a long, silent moment at the severed head. Then, reverently, he bowed. When he stood back up to his full height, Judith saw he was smiling. Before the women could say or do anything, however, he turned toward the forest and slipped into its shadows.

Nerienda looked down again. She couldn't believe what the girl had done. She knew that killing Holofernes was Judith's only option, but she hadn't expected her to march out of the tent carrying a bloody head at her side.

Nerienda threw the contents of their bag on the ground and opened it wide so Holofernes's head could fit inside. There was no need to carry it all the way back to town exposed. Then she threw Judith's cloak over the girl's shoulders and pulled her along their pre-planned escape route.

"Wait," Judith said. She bent down in the dim light of the abandoned campfires and looked at all the contents of their bag scattered on the ground. She was just able to make out the object she wanted. Carefully, she wiped the blood from her hand as best she could and picked up the little doll. She tucked it into one of the pockets inside her cloak, safe from the spatters of blood. Then she reached out for Nerienda's hand, and the two women set out at a run for home.

Nerienda could feel the girl shaking, but she did not dare stop. She only prayed that whatever was causing Judith's trembling might not hinder them from returning home. It wasn't until they reached the edge of the large clearing that separated Holofernes's camp from Bethulia's walls that Nerienda paused to rest.

The moon was low in the sky. Dawn was nearing, but the waning moon still gave off plenty of light. Nerienda finally turned to look at Judith. She was astounded by what she saw. Back at camp, the light was dim, and her old eyes could only make out the outlines of Judith and Acwel. Here in the moonlight, she able to study the girl in detail. Judith was covered in blood; her dress was stained red, as were her hands and face. Her cloak had slipped off her shoulders. And, most shockingly, her head was completely uncovered. *And Acwel saw her like this.*

While they stood there catching their breath, Nerienda set to work. She pulled the maiden's cloak over her shoulders and clasped it securely so the garment covered her ripped bodice and provided warmth. Then she gingerly took the veil from Judith's hand. In a matter of a few moments, it was back on the maiden's head, securely in place. As long as no one looked too closely at the few visible bloodstains, Judith looked well put together.

Nerienda was ready to move on. She grabbed Judith's arm once more and tried to nudge her along, but the girl was in shock. She wouldn't move.

"Judith, everything is alright. You did well. You did exceptionally well, but it is time to go home."

Judith nodded but was unable to speak. Without warning, she collapsed into Nerienda's arms. The old woman held her for a few minutes, letting her regain her composure as best she could.

"He didn't hurt you, did he?" she asked with concern.

"No," Judith whispered. "He barely touched me."

"Good," Nerienda said. "Judith, we need to be going. Dawn is coming, and we cannot be out in the open when it arrives."

Judith wiped the tears from her eyes. First light was just beginning to break, and the two women could already see Bethulia before them; the open clearing was all that was left of their journey.

They were just beginning to feel some relief when somebody shouted at them from behind. They stopped and froze. Neither of them knew they were being followed. Slowly they turned and came face to face with Rowe. He was only a few feet from them, trying to be brave, standing there with a small dagger pointed toward the women.

"Don't take another step," he gasped. He had obviously been running to catch up with them. "I know what you've done. I saw the whole thing. I know how to hide in the shadows too. You have his head. You must give it back. We must bury it with the body."

Nerienda was about to say something, but Judith reacted first.

"No. We can't. We won't. We must take it back with us."

The boy moved closer. Fear flashed in his eyes and clouded his judgment. He was confused and trying desperately to fix a situation that could not be mended. "Don't worry," he said, turning to Judith. "Toland can lead us. He can be lord to us just as well as Holofernes, and you can be his queen instead."

Nerienda and Judith looked at each other. Rowe was getting louder, and they did not want to rouse a sleeping army. Had they completed such a horrendous task only to have a frightened child stop them in the final stage of their plans? Judith was still trembling with shock, but Nerienda stepped forward.

"Listen, boy," she said. "You have one of two options. Either come with us and live in our town, where you will be taken care of, or stay here and be killed."

Rowe looked at them defiantly, his courage beginning to grow. "No, I'm not going with you. This is where I belong now, and I can't leave. And you can't go either. If you turn and walk away, I will be forced to kill you."

The boy was clearly scared. The dagger shook in his outstretched hand. Nerienda walked forward, trying to calm him.

"Take a deep breath, my dear. Everything will be fine. Just come with us, and all will be well."

Nerienda inched closer, but Rowe stood his ground. All the while, Judith stood frozen in place, but there was a soft thud as the doll from her pocket fell to the ground. Rowe flinched at the motion. His eyes grew wide at the sight of the doll.

"Mayda?" he whispered and looked at the two women with alarm.

It took only a moment for him to regain his voice. "Where did you find that?" he screamed as he tried to lunge forward, but Nerienda caught him before he could take a step.

She grabbed the dagger, but the boy screamed and fought back. He kicked her shin and beat his fists against her back. Nerienda dodged the worst of the blows, then with one swift move, she dug his blade deep into his gut while her other hand covered his mouth to stifle his cries. Rowe collapsed in her arms. Nerienda felt his life leaving him.

"I'm sorry," she whispered into his ear. "But it had to be done. It's better this way. You'll be at peace now with your family."

Nerienda held the child in her arms until he was dead. At least the boy was finally free from the barbarians who had enslaved him. Nerienda folded Rowe's arms across his chest and made the sign of the cross over his body. She left the scop and his dagger where she hoped the army would recognize his bravery and give him a proper burial. Then she looked at Judith, trembling.

"Two men and a boy in one night. That's far too much death for me. Come, Judith, let's go home."

***

Time was of the essence. Judith and Nerienda were racing against their enemy, hoping against hope that none of the thanes would stir before they reached safety. Their quickest route home was the open meadow, and if they had to cross it in daylight, they would surely be seen.

After leaving Rowe where he died, it took just a few more moments before they were out in the open and running as fast as they could. They held hands and helped one another along. When one stumbled, the other would pick her back up without losing speed. There was no time to think about what had happened over the past few hours, no time to give thought to what they carried with them. All they could do was run.

I'm flying, Judith thought. *I'm flying back to Bethulia.* She laughed out loud as she instinctively raised her hand to her neck to make sure her precious bird necklace was still safely secured.

As the women pressed on, trying to beat the sun, Judith had full view of the sky as it transformed from inky black to a rosy dawn. It seemed the sun was running a race of its own as if it had never been more anxious to herald in the day. The night clouds dispersed and rays of light broke through their cracks. The horizon came alive with vibrant oranges, reds, pinks, and royal purples.

Squirrels started their chattering and shadows glided easily at the forest's edge. *Deer*, she thought upon seeing the rustling of the shrubs. Hedgehogs, badgers, and small foxes were heading home for bed while the rabbits were just beginning to stick their noses into the morning air to see if it was safe to venture out. As the women came upon the last stretch of the journey, a choir of songbirds started their cacophonous music.

Suddenly, she heard the piercing call of large black birds circling high above the trees. She stopped in her tracks. "Ravens," she cried.

She could just make out the birds, distant yet unmistakable, soaring over the crest of the horizon, beating their mighty wings. She could hear the low growls of the wolves as they paced on calloused paws within the shadows of the forest. She felt as alive as the new day and could hear her pulse pounding in her head like a drum as the signs of impending bloodshed gathered around her.

The guards stationed at Bethulia's gate watched the women as they approached. Anticipating an enemy, they braced themselves for a fight. But as Judith and Nerienda drew closer, they saw the travelers were women, and both seemed to have a familiar appearance.

It was Bearn who noticed Judith's golden hair glistening in the first rays of sunlight. Her head was covered, but the end of her hair lay over her shoulder and reached past her veil. Judith kept to herself in the city, but the wisps of blonde that always managed to escape the corners of her veil matched her braid's color perfectly. Meanwhile, Erian recognized Nerienda. There was no mistaking the slight stature and unique gait of the old woman, who could often be seen walking around town.

The guards were confused as to how the women had escaped from the city, and they were hesitant to open the gate. Always on the defense, they feared the women's arrival might be a trap, though both men had to admit it seemed unlikely there was anyone else around.

The women drew closer until they finally reached the city gate, where they fell to the ground exhausted and gasping for air. Only Judith had enough breath left to cry out, "Let us in. Let us back into the city."

CHAPTER 24

Cyneric had been watching and waiting these past few days. It had been three nights since Judith's departure, and he was beginning to despair. Anxious and scared, he worried night and day about what might come next. If Judith and Nerienda failed, all would be lost. He knew there was no way he could defeat Holofernes in his first battle as commander. So, he prayed, and without giving away any details, he encouraged the townspeople to pray as well. "Deliverance. Pray for deliverance. Pray for salvation." And they did. Men, women, and children—all prayed their town would be spared.

The young lord had spent another restless night plagued with worry. While it was still dark out, he left his quarters and started pacing the city walls. At dawn, the town was still asleep. Even the birds nesting within Bethulia's limits had yet to start chirping in fervor.

Cyneric was not far from the gate when a shout arose from the other side. He couldn't hear who it was or what they were saying. He couldn't even tell if it was a man or a woman, but he hoped and prayed it might be Judith. He ran to the guard's tower and stood at the base.

"Who is it? Who's there?" he called up toward his men.

The two men looked down at him, puzzled.

"It's Judith and her maid," Bearn called down.

"Open the gate. Open the gate immediately," Cyneric shouted.

"But, my lord," Erian said, "perhaps it's a trap."

The lord looked at them. "Is anyone with them?"

"No," they said in unison.

"Ask her if she was victorious," Cyneric ordered.

Still puzzled, the guards looked at each other before Bearn shouted down. "The lord wants to know, my lady, if you were victorious."

Judith looked up and gave a tired smile. "Yes. Yes, we were."

"Let her in at once," Cyneric shouted. "Hurry, there is no time to lose."

The two guards descended from their towers. The gate had not been opened in months, and the wood had swelled in its hold. After a few attempts, the timbers were loosened. With their strength multiplied by the adrenaline coursing through their veins, the three men moved the logs to the side – normally a task requiring half a dozen men. They pulled the heavy gate open only far enough for Cyneric and Bearn to go out to meet the women.

When Cyneric saw the smile on Judith's face, he gave a loud cheer and embraced her. The women were out of breath, weak from the run, and exhausted from lack of sleep. They leaned heavily against the men, who helped them through the narrow opening. As soon as they were inside, the men shut and barred the doors once again.

Once the gates were secure, everyone took a moment to catch their breath. Then Cyneric calmly commanded the guards to awaken everyone and send them all immediately to the mead hall. There was no time to lose. The townspeople needed to be gathered as quickly as possible.

The men set out at once, but Cyneric stayed back with Judith and Nerienda, helping them to the mead hall. It wasn't as large as Holofernes's tent, but it was big enough to hold the small population that dwelled within the walls of the town. As they walked with their lord, Judith and Nerienda told Cyneric everything that had happened in the time they were gone. He listened carefully to their story and spoke only after they were done.

"Well done, Judith, and thank you. I knew I was right in trusting you. Now that you have succeeded, I will lead our army this very morning to Holofernes's camp to defeat his men. First, though, we must speak to the townspeople of all that has happened."

They arrived at the mead hall long before anyone else. "Bring us bread, water, mead, and any meat that might be on hand," Cyneric ordered.

The food arrived after only a moment, and the two famished women ate quickly. Within a quarter of an hour, the townspeople gathered. The children were still half asleep, and their mothers were worried. The fathers, thanes, elders, tradesmen—everyone looked confused and anxious. As the people settled in, Cyneric stood at the front of the hall and began to speak.

"For five months now, our town has been under siege. Holofernes's army has waged war on the entire country. All towns north of us have been destroyed. We saw the destruction of our neighbors only a few miles from us on the night my father, our great lord, died.

"I knew that if our town was to have any hope of surviving, we needed to destroy the leader of the enemy army. But I'd heard from travelers and woodsmen that there was not a single army out there strong enough to defeat Holofernes and his men. Every time someone tried, they were cut down. The army killed every loyal thane, butchered every lord, and defiled and murdered every woman and child. These men have done unspeakable acts, and though we have lived on little food, I was not going to allow anyone to set foot outside this town until we had a chance at victory. All our provisions have been coming to us through a side passage known only to myself, Bronson, our blacksmith, and a few trusted farmers. No Bethulian has entered or exited this city in five months, except Judith."

Judith stood in the shadows toward the front of the room, but as Cyneric called her name, Nerienda gave her a shove forward. With eyes downcast, she stood in front of her people, bloody and disheveled. Cyneric turned in her direction, and the townspeople gasped at her appearance. She was a mess, with her bloodstained hands and her wispy hair escaping her veil. Her cloak had slipped off her shoulder again, and her torn bodice was now visible.

"Several nights ago," Cyneric continued, "I came to Judith with a plan. 'Our last hope,' I told her, 'is that you leave our city walls in the veil of night and travel to the enemy camp.' Once there, she was instructed to convince Lord Holofernes that she and her maid meant no harm and needed a place to stay. After gaining the man's trust, they were to find a way to kill him."

As soon as the words left his mouth, Cyneric saw horror and fear spread through the room.

"I wasn't sure if Judith would return victorious," he continued. "I knew this task was dangerous and the odds were against her. But I also knew this town's great faith—and Judith's most of all. She is young and beautiful, and she prays more than anyone I know. That's why I sent her. Judith," he said as he gestured for her to continue the story.

Judith finally looked out over the crowd, and with the eloquence of her father, she began.

"We arrived at Holofernes's camp four mornings ago with the help of a woodsman. We were discovered almost immediately and had to pretend Nerienda was injured. Our story was that we had been running for days, trying to escape a cruel lord. Once we convinced the guards we were telling the truth, Nerienda was carried off to see the doctor, and I was led to Holofernes.

"He was a large, intimidating man, but he was intrigued by me. Though he was wary at our arrival, he gave us a tent of our own and invited me to have dinner with him that first night. It was at dinner that he invited us to stay the night with his army.

"Over the next few days, we spent quite a bit of time together. I learned as much about him as I could. The man was desperate for companionship, and he offered Nerienda and me the privilege of staying with his army throughout their remaining travels and asked me to be his queen once we returned to the north."

Many of the townspeople began to whisper, but Judith paid no attention.

"I said yes."

Immediately, the murmurs grew louder.

"I knew," she continued confidently, "that if I denied his proposal, he would kill me, or at the very least grow suspicious of my intentions. Besides, the agreement offered me protection from the other men, and there was a real need for that.

"Last night, Holofernes hosted a great feast for his men. While we starved behind our city walls, the army outside was getting ready for a huge celebration. The feast ran long into the night. In addition to the food and mead, there were hours of songs, stories, and countless gifts bestowed on Holofernes's thanes. The men became drunk and many passed out before the feast was over.

"Yesterday afternoon, I spoke with Holofernes once again, and we agreed that I would see him in his own quarters after the feast was over."

At this, the hushed whispers stopped, and everyone stared in amazement that Judith was both brave enough to admit this and that she had agreed to it.

"Nerienda and I made a poison, and I had plans to pour it into his drink. However, our plans did not go as we hoped. The guard who came to meet me found the poison and destroyed it. Then he tried to take me into an abandoned tent for himself. God blessed us, though, and Nerienda was able to kill him before he had a chance."

The townspeople turned toward Nerienda with quiet honor. The old woman stood proudly, if not slightly hunched over, in the corner.

"After that, we made our way to Holofernes's tent on our own. There were only two options for us now. I was either to succeed at the task Lord Cyneric had given me, or Nerienda and I would die in the morning when the guard's body was discovered.

"I waited in Holofernes's tent for him. When he entered, he was drunk. He passed out on the bed, sound asleep before he had a chance to lay a hand on me. I made sure he was unconscious, then I used his own sword against him. I sliced his neck through in two strokes."

Judith's audience was captivated. Every man, woman, and child of Bethulia stared at her in silence. She motioned for Nerienda to step forward with the bag.

"If the blood on my clothes and body is not enough to prove I have killed our greatest enemy, then look upon his face yourself."

Nerienda grasped a clump of Holofernes's greasy hair, pulled the severed head from the bag, and held it up for everyone to see. Most of the head was matted with blood, but the face was still distinguishable. Everyone knew the rumors that Holofernes was the dark lord of the north, and his features lived up to their reputation. Holofernes was the only full-blooded Celt to rule the

Angles and Saxons.

Nerienda handed the head to Judith and quietly stepped back into the corner.

"Here he is," Judith said. "The lord of the enemy army. Destroyed and defeated. While his head is here, his body lies in his tent miles away."

The townspeople were shocked and disgusted at the sight. They could not believe that sweet, innocent Judith had accomplished such an act of savagery.

"We are saved," Judith continued, "but only if the men of this town can rise up and go and defeat this enemy. Lord Holofernes is dead. His greatest warrior is also dead, and the rest of the men are, as far as we know, still sound asleep in a drunken stupor. You must have courage. You must defeat them. Otherwise, they will continue to wreak havoc on our country, and our town will be the next to be destroyed."

At this, Judith looked to Cyneric, who stepped up beside her. He nodded at Judith, gratitude shining in his eyes. Then he looked toward his people and began to speak.

"We have the advantage now. They are vulnerable. Go, grab your armor, your swords, axes, and every weapon you have. We will destroy them. They are neither ready nor fit to fight. From a young age we were taught to fight honorably in battle when both sides are prepared and ready. This will not be an honorable battle, but these men have never fought honorably, and we seek victory not just for ourselves but for all those they have killed."

The Bethulians cheered, and Cyneric waited for them to quiet.

"Judith has taken down our greatest enemy. It is time for us to scatter his herd of sheep. They have destroyed thousands of innocent lives. Now we must avenge them. Let no enemy warrior escape. Kill every one of them. Today they shall meet their lord in the afterlife."

The people began to chant even louder, but Cyneric continued.

"We will open the gates and march forward with Holofernes's head on a pike. Let this be the first thing his men see as we near their camp. Then when the war horn bellows, roar as loud as you can, bang your swords against your shields, and raise a noise that will frighten and confuse even the bravest of them. They will be caught off guard and unprepared for battle.

"Now go and get ready. Every able-bodied man is to meet me at the gate."

The men left, but Cyneric continued to give orders, turning his attention now to the women.

"Combine all of the flour we have, start making bread for everyone so our people can eat when we return triumphant. Do not spare even an ounce of wheat. I promise that by the day's end we will be able to eat in abundance again."

Finally, Cyneric looked back to Judith. The love he had always felt for her nearly overwhelmed him now, and he wanted nothing more than to wrap his arms around her and keep her for himself forever.

"You have done more than enough," he said. "I know Holofernes asked you to be his queen, but after we are victorious today, I will humbly ask you to be mine instead."

Judith smiled at Cyneric. She had a hard time realizing this man standing before her was the same man she had known all her life, the one who shared so many of her childhood memories, stories, and secrets from years ago. But Cyneric's eyes convinced her. His eyes weren't dark and mysterious. They were bright and clear. No flame was lit within her when she looked at her old friend. Instead, her whole heart burst with the love that had always been there.

She was unsure how a feat she had conducted in near solitude had brought her so close to Cyneric once more. It would be years before she understood that she and Nerienda hadn't been alone on their journey. Cyneric had been with them every step of the way. He never told her, but he spent most of his days and nights on her roof in prayer while Judith was gone. He vowed that if the angels ever brought her back to him, he would never let her feel alone again.

Judith knew Cyneric wanted to give her the very thing she had been searching for all these years—a place to call home. In an instant, she realized that home was really the people she loved, those who were always with her. She hadn't understood that her best friend had been home to her just as much as her father. *Home,* she thought, *is not an escape from these walls. Home is being with the people I care about. The ones who love me even when I doubt myself.*

With tears in her eyes, Judith gave a genuine smile and whispered with sincere gratitude, "I would be honored to be your queen."

Cyneric departed to prepare for battle. Judith was turning to leave, to take up her part in the preparations, when she saw Nerienda. The old woman was still standing in the corner, looking weary and worn. Judith sent her home to wash up and go to bed. Nerienda tried to protest, but she was grateful to be relieved of her duties. The two women set off together—one for their small home and the other for the city gates.

By the time Judith arrived at the gate, a large group of men had gathered, but many more were still on their way. Cyneric walked toward the front of the group as one of his thanes ran behind him, fastening his last bit of armor. The lord carried his helmet under his arm and his father's sword at his side. Seeing Judith as he neared the open gate, he approached her.

"What are you doing here?" he asked as concern creased his face. "Go home. Go to bed. You have done more than enough for us."

Judith shook her head. "I can't simply go to sleep while you and the men fight a war that I began. At least let me watch from the tower so I can see all that's happening and pray for our city's victory."

Looking beneath her tired and weary face, Cyneric saw that her request was fervent. He gave a nod and led Judith to the tower and helped her climb to the top. She took up her new position, anxious for the battle to begin.

CHAPTER 25

The open meadow was long, and the men had a great march ahead of them. Judith was sure their war cry and beating drums would reach Holofernes's men long before the Bethulians arrived. She suspected the enemy soldiers would have enough time to find their lord deceased and make hasty battle preparations but not enough time to plan an attack, not with Holofernes gone.

From her vantage point, Judith could just make out the outline of the enemy camp resting peacefully at the edge of the meadow with the forest behind it. Five eagles circled and a pack of wolves emerged from the forest. Soon after, the flock of ravens she had seen only a few hours before was joined by countless others flying in from every direction. This time, relief washed over her when she saw the trio of war beasts. There was finally going to be a battle. The Bethulians were ready, she and Nerienda were safe, and victory was almost certain.

"Open the gates," Cyneric shouted as he raised his sword.

The gates were drawn open, and two war horns blared through the morning air. The wolves at the forest's edge paced back and forth. They were ravenous.

***

The horns' loud cry echoed through the valley and reached the ears of Holofernes's men. Shouts, cheers, and even thunder could not have stirred them. However, they knew the call of war. They were trained to respond immediately whenever it sounded. With groggy eyes, they rose from their sleep. Most were confused, trying to figure out what was going on. Who had sounded the call for battle? From the comfort of camp, it didn't appear that there was imminent danger around them.

Toland was one of the first to arise. Confused by the distant sound, but not wanting to disturb Holofernes and Judith, he went first to look for Knut. When he couldn't find him, he went to Beartwold and the other advisors to see if they knew what was happening. The old men were just as perplexed as everyone else. They had not given the order for battle, and it appeared no one in camp knew who did. Finally, Toland and the elders went to Holofernes's tent, hoping that their lord could shed light on what was unfolding around them.

Not wanting to intrude on whatever might be happening in their lord's tent, the small group of men cleared their throats and coughed. They tried desperately to make themselves known discreetly. When their attempts seemed futile, the advisors looked at each other and then nudged Toland inside.

"My lord," Toland said as he stumbled through the entrance, shielding his eyes. "A war horn has sounded, but we don't know who it came from." He was looking down at the ground, not wanting to interrupt. He stood that way for some seconds, waiting for a response. In those silent moments, he noticed the dark stains on the dirt floor. Slowly Toland looked up to address his lord.

"My lord—" he started again, but his sentence was cut short. The gold curtain that had been drawn around the bed in the middle of the night was now thrown open. There before him, sprawled across the bed, was Holofernes's body covered in blood. It took a few moments for Toland to understand the scene and a few more to notice that Holofernes's head was missing.

Toland shouted for the others. When the elders entered and saw their lord dead and dismembered, they began to panic. They got down on their hands and knees and searched every inch of the tent, but there was no sign of the head anywhere.

Confused and afraid, they all frantically tried to surmise who could have done such a thing. One of them suggested that someone might have snuck in, kidnapped Judith, and killed their lord, but the men knew of no enemies in the area. They had killed everyone who might have followed them south. It wasn't until one of the advisors noticed the necklace Holofernes had gifted Judith just inside the tent's entrance that they began to piece together the truth.

"Could it be?" one man asked. "Could she have killed him?"

Toland felt a sense of dread wash over him. "She's done this!" he cried before anyone else could answer the question. "She tricked him. She tricked all of us." Everything he had feared when Judith first arrived seemed to have come true. He despaired that he had not followed his suspicions and stopped Judith. He had failed his commander.

While the men were slowly reconstructing the events from the night before, another war horn sounded from much closer, clearly coming from the south.

"They are coming for us," Toland said to the small party. The Bethulians had outsmarted them.

The thanes throughout the army were now fully awake, and they started to grow anxious as the battle calls grew louder. Since no orders had been given, most of the soldiers started making their way toward the center of camp. They congregated outside the mead hall and insisted on seeing their lord.

When Toland and the advisors saw the army gathering, they stepped out of Holofernes's tent to address the crowd. Toland was unanimously elected to share the dire news with the whole army. The advisors elbowed him toward the mead hall entrance. Reluctantly, he stood on a table in full view of everyone. It took some moments for him to gather his thoughts, but when he finally opened his mouth to speak, the words came rushing out.

"My brothers," his voice cracked as he began. "You all know the many victories we have experienced during our years of travel. Together, under the guidance of our Lord Holofernes, we have conquered every town, army, and lord we have come across. We have seen many fall under our swords. We have been showered with triumphs and gifts beyond our imagining, and the legend of our deeds will live on for generations. But every journey must come to an end."

Toland's voice cracked again. His hands began to tremble with fear. Never one to show emotion, he fought hard to steady himself and continue. Looking the men square in the eyes, he spoke more calmly.

"It appears we have all been tricked, our lord most of all, by the beauty of a young maiden." There were a few murmurs in the crowd as the men began to search for Judith. "As most of you know, Judith, the woman who has been with us these past few days, was supposed to spend the night with our lord. But it appears her intentions were not what they seemed. This morning the advisors and I found our dear lord lying in his bed covered with blood, beheaded."

Shouts, cries, and angry slurs filled the air. The army pushed closer to Holofernes's tent as they tried to fight their way inside.

He pressed on, shouting over the commotion. "I have no doubt Judith was sent to us as a spy from Bethulia, and now the city has finally opened its gates. You have heard the war horn sound in the distance. They are coming to attack us."

The men fell silent. Toland once again had their complete attention.

"Our lord is dead, of that we are certain. His story has ended, but we can continue what we started. We can be remembered as the army who accomplished more in our lord's honor than we ever did while he was alive! Who will fight with me for the honor of our lord? Who will see to it that we are victorious once again despite our great loss? Who will help me conquer this army and ravage this city until every timber of their beloved wall has been burned to the ground?"

Stirred by Toland's passion, the men cheered mightily.

"Go now and prepare for battle. The army will soon be upon us, but we will be ready for them. We are stronger, braver, and more worthy of victory than they ever will be. We will destroy them. And when they are defeated, we will see to it that their lord suffers a worse fate than ours."

With one last battle cry, the men scattered and began to prepare for yet another fight. However, without the direction of Holofernes, many of them felt less confident than their cries led their companions to believe. Instead of feeling stirred to battle, most of the soldiers secretly felt relief and even freedom at Holofernes's demise. Though it was never spoken of, all had witnessed his barbaric displays of anger and secretly worried it would one day be directed at them.

Those who did feel honor-bound had only been loyal out of

fear. A true lord is loved by his thanes because he loves them first. Holofernes had never loved any of them, and now that the fear had passed, they realized they no longer felt any allegiance toward the man who had dragged them away from their families and forced them to kill innocent men, women, and children. Confused and uncertain, many of the soldiers packed up what few necessities they could carry and planned to flee before the battle began.

As the camp spun into chaos, one of the advisors went to investigate Judith's tent. To his horror, he found no trace of the women, only Knut lying dead and bloody in the dirt. Only moments later, three thanes came upon the lifeless body of the scop. The news of the deaths spread like wildfire.

"Those two women are heartless."

"They are murderers!"

"They betrayed us all."

The war horn blew one last time. The bellowing blast was so close now that the entire camp heard the accompanying war cries. The thunderous pounding of shields confirmed that the Bethulian soldiers were nearly upon them. Panicked by the approaching army, most soldiers turned to flee. The few men who wanted to fight secured their armor and moved to the southernmost end of the camp.

As the Bethulians crested the final hill and barreled down the meadow, the panicked thanes realized their only escape was through the forest, where the hungry wolves lurked. Even from camp they could hear their low growls and guttural threats. Fighting off packs of wolves in the dark woods was even more of a risk than fighting an army in an open field. If they defeated the army, there was at least a chance they could return home as a group, better equipped to fend off the threats in the woods. They dropped their belongings and begrudgingly prepared for battle.

They made their way toward the south end of the camp and stood on the front lines, afraid of what was to come next.

As the two armies converged, Judith stood back at the tower watching the entire scene. Holofernes's men were scattered and confused. She sent one final petition to heaven with the hopes that the men of Bethulia would be courageous and valiant enough to secure a victory over the undefeated army they were about to face.

CHAPTER 26

A s the advancing army marched forward with Cyneric leading the way, Holofernes's men spotted something high above their heads. They brandished a round object on a wooden pike. It did not take much imagination to realize it was Holofernes's head. A shudder of terror swept through the army. Men started running in every direction. Hopeless, they darted toward the forest, praying one way or another the woods would help them disappear forever.

Cyneric watched the enemy army carefully. As the men scattered, he gave the signal to attack. With a mighty roar from the Bethulians and a swift push forward, the battle began. Swords clashed, iron hit iron, and shouts of defeat and victory echoed across the clearing. Few of Holofernes's men made it to the forest's edge before they were butchered. Those that did manage to escape into the woods were soon hunted down like animals and left for dead.

From her perch on the high tower, Judith watched the whole scene. Even at such a great distance, she could see the men fought bravely. Swords impaled the chests of enemy soldiers. Heads flew through the air with one stroke of an axe. Soldiers fell as their entrails spilled on the ground.

As the battle raged on, Toland's gold helmet was clearly visible.

If there was anyone who could rally the troops and lead them to victory, it was Toland. She wanted to be sure he was killed even if others survived. About midway through the battle, she finally saw his gold helmet fall to the ground; it didn't rise up again. Bearn's sword pierced Toland's gut, and Holofernes's most loyal thane collapsed as blood gushed from his abdomen. With a swift turn of his heel, Bearn ventured into the sea of tents to search out those who had been too afraid to meet them at the camp's edge. Judith said a half-hearted prayer for Toland's soul before turning her attention back to the battlefield to make sure Cyneric was still standing.

The young lord seemed to be outfighting his most talented warriors. He was strong and unwavering. Judith felt her pulse quicken as she watched him skillfully fell one enemy soldier after another. Judith knew he had been scared to take up his new position as lord, especially with Holofernes camped outside the gates of the city, but he more than made up for his cowardice on the battlefield. He led the army like a true commander—with wisdom far beyond his years.

The sun rose high into the sky, and Cyneric shouted encouragement to his men above the roar of the battle. "Fear not. Just a few more hours of strength and bravery, and our enemy will be defeated. Keep going. Stay strong. You can see the wolves, ravens, and eagles circling above and around us. Let's make sure that they feast on the bodies of our enemies tonight."

The men rallied at his words. Holofernes's soldiers were so skilled they were able to follow their training despite their stupor, even without their commander. Yet, the Bethulian army responded in turn, proving to be more adept at offensive maneuvers and defensive formations than the still inebriated enemy.

Judith recognized a few friends amongst the men fighting. Olaf had led the chase against those who tried to flee the battlefield and hide in the forest. From a distance he looked like a great bear fighting on two legs. *If there is anyone who can track down those men, it is undoubtedly Olaf,* Judith thought as his large, fur-trimmed silhouette disappeared into the woods.

She spied Bronson leading the second string of laymen and farmers who had volunteered for battle. Though these men were not trained in fighting, they made up for their lack of technique with courage. Bronson wielded an ax and moved to engage the enemy in close combat. With one swift motion, he lodged the ax into the man's side and the thane fell to the ground, dead. *He must have forged the ax blade himself,* she thought. *If it is as strong and sharp as the dagger he gave me, one swing to a man's side would easily prove fatal.*

Judith watched the entire battle, refusing to take her eyes off it even once. Throughout the day, Nerienda arrived several times to check on the girl. She made sure Judith ate and drank, passing up small pieces of bread and cups of mead or water every few hours. Judith dutifully took what Nerienda offered and forced herself to finish every bite. Even though the maiden hadn't even changed her bloody clothes yet, and there were still a few smudges of Holofernes's blood on the backs of her hands and face, she refused to abandon her post and the men who were fighting for the city. Instead, she continued to stand and pray while Nerienda kept watch below.

Every man in the Bethulian army fought nobly—lord, thane, and farmer alike. They fought together, giving their sweat and blood for their city. The last of Holofernes's men fell just before dusk, and as the sun set, Cyneric and his army returned to the city weary and wounded, but happy. Even more miraculous than the victory was that not a single Bethulian had been lost. Every man returned home to his family and friends that day.

None of the enemy soldiers survived the battle. By nightfall, Holofernes's great army, which had tormented and ransacked the entire northern half of the country, was no more. The impenetrable, undefeated, and unrelenting army was destroyed at the hands of a beautiful maiden, a young lord, and a starving city.

CHAPTER 27

As the Bethulians returned home, they were cheered and celebrated. Even those who lived outside the high walls made their way to the town to await the return of the victorious army. Cyneric waited until he was sure every last one of his men had returned safely before he entered the gates. When he did, he was met with celebration, music, and shouts of joy.

As the town erupted in cries of victory, Cyneric saw Judith standing right where he had left her that morning, at the gate, watching over the men who had been out on the field. He gestured to her, signaling that she deserved as much honor as anyone.

"Judith," the town shouted in unison. They had her to thank for their salvation. It was her courage that had led them to victory.

The jubilant cries grew even louder as Cyneric motioned for her to descend from the tower. The lord helped her down the last few steps, making sure she landed safely. Once her feet were firmly on the ground, Cyneric took her hand in his and knelt ceremoniously on one knee before her.

The chanting crowd grew silent, and everyone knelt in honor. Then their chanting began again. This time, however, they shouted, "Idesse. Idesse."

Idesse. Fairy-like, more than queen, not quite a goddess. The title was an honor above all others. With tears in her eyes, she looked out over the crowd and gave a slight bow to her people.

Finally, she understood that the Bethulians had always been her people, and she loved them. It seemed clear now that her call to serve them was the one thing in her life that would never change. Judith was filled with peace and joy. She felt a newfound appreciation for her role in this world. She was finally home.

As the townspeople cheered Judith on and bowed before her, Nerienda stood off to the side and gave her own bow. She was as proud of Judith as any mother would have been. While the townspeople saw a heroic queen before them, the old maid's heart swelled with pride that, despite her temptations, Judith had chosen the most noble path.

Judith's eyes found Nerienda, always faithful, standing off to the side. She bowed her head to Nerienda. The two women had been through something no one else had experienced. Their journey bonded them for eternity in a way that nothing else could. In a matter of moments, Judith's family had grown to hundreds, but Nerienda was the only one who had always been by her side.

After a long while, Cyneric and his new queen led the men and women to the mead hall. Since there was no longer any threat of danger, the gates of Bethulia were left open, and inhabitants from the surrounding farms and forests came to join in the celebration. There were no outcasts tonight; everyone was welcome. The mead hall had never been so full, but somehow, there was enough room for everyone.

Once the hall was filled and everyone settled, the music and singing began. It was a true feast—filled with joy, peace, happiness, and hope for the future. Despite the hasty preparation, the food was as delicious as the meal Holofernes had provided his men. The women in the town had been hard at work cooking the meal during the battle. They'd emptied their stores of all their best spices and produce and slaughtered many of the animals that remained in the town. Neighbors from the south who had heard the city gates were opened once more rushed in to offer whatever food they could. By the end of the day, there was enough for an army twice the size of Holofernes's and plenty leftover to help the Bethulians through the next several months while they worked to produce their own harvest.

Cyneric stood up and motioned to silence his guests. He called the scops forward and asked them to tell the story of the battle they had just won. Two musicians stood and played a few chords on their harps. Taking turns, they sang the story of the time when Judith slayed the monster, Lord Holofernes, and Lord Cyneric and the Bethulians destroyed the unbeatable northern army. The song was lively and the imagery as vivid as the actual events. The tune lasted a long while and seemed to carry the listeners away with it as they sat enraptured by the tale.

When it was over, one final cheer rose before everyone departed, heading home to their own beds to sleep. Each person left feeling content, knowing the great danger that had stood outside the city walls was gone. They could rest peacefully.

Judith returned to her humble home, escorted by Lord Cyneric. As they said goodnight to one another, Cyneric stared into her eyes as deeply as Holofernes had, as if he was looking past her physical beauty and straight into her soul. It was a look Cyneric had never given her, and yet it seemed so familiar. The lord brushed her cheek softly with his thumb and then gave her a small kiss on the corner of her mouth.

"There will be a wedding soon," Cyneric said, "and I look forward to it."

"I do too," Judith smiled. The weight of the past few days fell heavily on her shoulders. All at once, she felt exhausted. *I might sleep for days*, she thought. Cyneric gave Judith one final embrace and felt her collapse in his arms. Then Nerienda, who had been listening from inside the hut, came out and helped a weak and weary Judith into their home.

Nerienda helped Judith prepare for bed. She cleaned the girl up as best she could in the dim candlelight. She helped her out of her stiff, blood-dried clothes and put her in a soft nightgown. Then she removed the girl's veil and carefully undid the intricate braid that was still surprisingly intact. After Nerienda had finished, she gently guided Judith over to the bed, where she fell into a deep, peaceful sleep.

***

All was well in Bethulia that night and for many nights to come. There was peace for the whole country. The air seemed lighter. The night sky seemed clearer. The heaviness that had rested on the city during the months of siege was finally lifted. Everyone felt relief.

Nerienda, happy to be home, climbed to the roof of their small hut where Judith spent so much of her time. With Judith safely asleep below her, she looked up at the sky and spent the night in prayer and thanksgiving. From the roof, she could hear the eagles, ravens, and wolves as they enjoyed their own feast. What a wild adventure her old bones had just been through! Never in all her years did she think her greatest journey would happen at the end of her life.

Nerienda knew that the future was still a mystery, but she was grateful that Judith had found a place in the town and happiness in the arms of a man who had proven his loyalty, courage, and bravery. Cyneric would lead his people well. Nerienda was happy knowing that even after she was gone, Judith would have many other people to love and cherish her just as much as she did. Ever since the two had been on their own, Nerienda had secretly prayed that, when the time came, there would be someone else to take her place and bring Judith a sense of family. For the first time in many years, her heart felt at peace.

EPILOGUE

The sun shone brightly on the expansive battlefield. The storm had passed. The war was over. The wolves, eagles, and ravens sulked in the shadows, waiting until nightfall to feast once again on the carrion left sitting in the sunlight. In daylight, the men of Bethulia marched out onto the battlefield to collect the treasures of their victory. And what a victory it was!

Though nearly a month had passed, the Bethulians were still gathering cartload after cartload of treasures and valuables. In addition to the gold and silver coins, there were adornments, armor, emeralds, rubies, garnets, pearls, sapphire, amber and sea glass set in rings, necklaces, bracelets, belt buckles, crowns, and sword hilts. They found the treasures stashed in chests and bags in the enemy tents standing furthest from the battlefield—just as Judith had said. The Bethulians were aware that the treasures had come from those pillaged towns and villages Holofernes's army had defeated before arriving at the gates of Bethulia. With each haul that was brought in, prayers were said for the deceased.

Back on the battlefield, gold chains, silver amulets, bronze armbands, and strong metal sword sheathes were found on Holofernes's men as they lay dead and half-devoured on the ground. They were so adorned in precious metals that the sun glistened off them, nearly blinding the Bethulians. The treasures were deposited in the town center, and the old women shined and polished the items until they sparkled from every angle. The younger women of the town organized the valuables into neat piles to be given in equal portion to every man who had fought or assisted the battle in some way. However, the rarest jewels, the most beautiful adornments, and Holofernes's own sword and armor were reserved for Judith, soon to be their queen.

The people of the town worked hard to clear the fields and organize their newfound wealth, but they refused to let Judith lift a finger to help. She spent her days walking back and forth between the town center and the large gates, where she watched the men on the field. Occasionally, she wandered through the streets and spent time with those who were too ill, too old, or too young to be of service.

One sunny afternoon as she was making her way back home, she caught sight of Ellette. The young girl was growing strong now, and she often reminded Judith of herself when she was little. The four-year-old was smiling at her behind her mother's skirt as they passed on the street. Judith knelt next to Ellette. Before Judith could speak, the sweet girl threw her arms around her neck.

"I am so happy you came back. I was worried while you were away," she squealed.

"How did you know I was gone?" Judith asked with a laugh.

"It'd been days since you climbed onto your roof," Ellette said matter-of-factly. "I knew you must have left when you didn't appear by the second morning." Ellette leaned in very closely and whispered in Judith's ear. "Don't worry. I didn't tell anyone."

Judith laughed louder as she returned the hug.

"Ellette, you have seen all the women cleaning the treasures in the center of town, haven't you?"

"Yes," she replied as she hopped back and forth from one foot to the other. "We are on our way to give Grandma her lunch right now. She is working there today."

"Well," Judith continued, "there is one more treasure that I brought back with me. I have been thinking long and hard about who to give it to, and I think you might be just the person to take care of it."

The little girl's eyes sparked with excitement, and she looked up to her mother. When her mother nodded, Ellette looked at Judith and gave a reassuring nod of approval as well.

Judith's smile broadened. "Could you wait one moment while I fetch it? It's just inside my house."

Judith disappeared and soon reappeared with the gift under her arm.

"I found this doll while I was away. She belonged to a little girl who cannot care for her anymore. She needs to be fixed up a bit, but I think she could be quite pretty once she is. Do you think you might be able to look after her?"

Ellette's sparkling green eyes grew wide. "Me?" she asked in wonderment.

"Yes," Judith replied. "She needs a good home with someone to take care of her. Do you think you are up for the job?"

"She is the most beautiful doll I have ever seen. Just look at her pretty eye," Ellette said as she gently took the doll from Judith and cradled it lovingly in her arms.

"I will take care of her until her first mommy comes back for her." After a moment of hesitation, Ellette asked, "What was her mommy's name?"

"Mayda," Judith said.

"Mayda," Ellette repeated softly. "Then that is what I will call her."

Judith smiled, and her eyes filled with tears. She saw that Ellette's mother was fighting back her own as she gave Judith a look of appreciation.

Judith watched the two walk away as Ellette sang a lullaby to her beautiful new doll. With a smile on her face, Judith turned back to her home, where she was supposed to be meeting Cyneric. When she caught sight of him, she ran to greet her lord and fiancé, and together they continued to the mead hall, where their marriage preparations were underway.

TRANSLATION

Translated[1] by Sarah Zilkowski with the assistance of Dr. Susan Kim, a professor at Illinois State University, using the Mitchell and Robinson Old English Text from *A Guide to Old English*, 6th ed.

Original Text found in the *Nowell Codex*.

1.   … doubt

2.   In this wide earth of gifts. She there readily found

3.   Hope of protection at the hands (of the) famous Prince when she had the greatest danger.

4.   The judge of grace called this that, he protected her with the highest terror.

5.   Protected, Lord of creatures. The Father in the sky is (him) he

6.   Glorious boon provided, she who had strong faith

7.   Always to the Almighty. Then I found out Holofernes was making eager to the

8.   Invitation of wine and all wondrous things sumptuous

9.   Dressing up a banquet, to them the lord of men commanded/called

10.   Then all (the) oldest thanes, that they with great haste

---

1 This translation follows the original text closely, preferring to keep the word order as close to the original as possible.

11.   Carried out shield-bearing warriors, came traveling to the powerful lord

12.   Reached, leader of the people. It was the 4th day

13.   After which Judith, wise in thought

14.   Woman beautiful as a fairy, first sought him.

15.   X Then they (the warriors) walked to the feast (and) sat,

16.   Proud to wine-drinking, all his companion in evil

17.   Bold mail-clad warriors. There was a cup,

18.   Brought frequently along the bench, also goblets and pitchers (flagons)

19.   Full with hall sitters; they that fate received

20.   Strong shield bearing warriors, yet the powerful one didn't expect
      (anything to happen)

21.   The terrible lord of Noblemen. Then was Holofernes,

22.   Lord of men, merry with drink;

23.   (He) laughed and bellowed, shouted and resounded

24.   That people (children) could hear from afar

25.   How the fierce (one) stormed and made a din

26.   Arrogant and drunk with mead, urged guests frequently

27.   That they should enjoy themselves thoroughly.

28.   So the wicked one over all the day

29.   Drenched his warriors with wine,

30.   Arrogant bestower of treasure, and until they lie dead in a swoon

31.   All his mature men inebriated they were also death stricken.

32.   Drained of every good thing. So called the lord of men,

33.   To be filled with hall guests for the children (people)

34.   The dark night draws near. The one with malice ordered

35.   The blessed woman to be fetched with haste

36.   To his bed, ring adorned,

37.   Ring adorned. They quickly did

38.   The servant, as their leader commanded them,

39.   Lord of mail clad warriors, instantly advanced

40. To the guest hall. There they found Judith

41. Prudent and then quickly the

42. Warriors began leading

43. The bright maiden to the high tent

44. Where the powerful man was always on the bed

45. Inside at night, hostile to the Savior,

46. Holofernes. There was all of gold a

47. Beautiful curtain and about the commander's

48. Bed hung that the evil (one)

49. Might look though, the warrior lord,

50. On each one of his sons which came inside there,

51. And on him none of mankind could look

52. Except the brave one. [Unless strong in malice who was ordered nearer to him

53. Of the warriors for getting a private consultation.]. Then they brought on a couch

54. Quickly the wise woman; then went Hard-hearted: heroes [that the holy woman was brought into his tent]

55. Warriors revealing to their lord that the holy woman was brought into the tent

56. Joyous, the nobleman of strongholds (Holofernes), then to the bright woman

57. He intended to corrupt with defilement and with polluting sin. The Judge of glory

58. Would not consent to that, the Guardian of majesty, but he prevented him from the deed,

59. Lord, Lord of mature men (seasoned warriors)

60. Then departed the diabolical

61. Lascivious warrior with troops of men

62. Evil (one) going to his bed, there he must lose his life

63. Immediately within one night; then reached his end

64. Violent on Earth, such an end as he had striven after previously

65. Fierce prince of men while he was in this world

66. Dwelt under the "cloud roof" (sky). He fell so drunk with wine

67. The powerful (one) upon his resting place so he did not know any advice

68. In mind. The warriors stepped

69. Out from the inside (of the tent) with great haste,

70. Men sated with wine, who led the scoundrel,

71. Hateful tyrant, to the bed

72. For the last time. Then was

73. The glorious handmaid of the Savior exceedingly concerned for her own self

74. How she could most easily deprive the terrible (one)

75. Of Life before the impure one, foul man awakened. (She) with braided hair, seized the man,

76. Maiden of the Creator, took a sharp sword,

77. Fierce from the storm of battle, and from its sheath drew it with

78. A mighty right hand; she began

79. To call by name the Guardian of Heaven, Savior of all

80. World dwellers, and uttered that word:

81. "I bid wish, you then, God of created things and Spirit of consolation,

82. Son of the Lord,

83. Mercy of thine to me in my need,

84. Glory of the Trinity. Severely now is my

85. Heart inflamed (burning) and mind sad,

86. With sorrows very stirred up. Grant me Prince of Heaven,

87. Victory and true faith, that I with this sword be allowed

88. To kill this bestower of the crime; grant me my success,

89. Fierce Prince of men.

90. Fierce Prince of men. (combined with lines above)

91.   I do not, have never needed your

92.   Mercy more than now.

93.   now, Mighty Lord

94.   Glorious bestower of glory, that is in this way grievously at my heart

95.   Burning within my heart." Then the highest Judge

96.   Immediately inspired her with courage so he does each one

97.   Of the dwellers on Earth

98.   Who seeks Him as a help to them in advise and true faith.

99.   Then He with an abundance in heart,

100. Restored hope with the holy woman; then she took the heathen man

101. Firmly by the hair, drew him toward her

102. Ignominiously, and the evil one

103. Skillfully laid out, hostile man,

104. As she was most easily able to control this wretched one

105. The one with braided hair struck

106. The enemy with a stained sword

107. Hateful one, that she cut through half

108. His neck that he lay in a swoon,

109. Drunk and wounded. He was not yet

110. Lifeless of all (dead yet); then struck earnestly the

111. Courageous woman

112. The heathen dog on the other side that his head rolled

113. Forth onto the floor. The foul torso lay

114. Behind dead; the spirit flew else wither

115. Under a deep chasm and there was prostrated,

116. Torment bound forever after,

117. Enveloped with worms (serpents), bound with punishment

118. Firmly held captive in hell-fire

119. After death. He had no need of hope,

120. Enwrapped in darkness, that thence he might

121. From the hall of serpents but there must dwell forever in the dark home

122. Without life

123. "Glory to the Lord of hosts who gave her honor Without end forever more."

124. XI Then Judith had won by fighting illustrious glory

125. At Battle, so her God granted,

126. Prince in heaven, who granted her victory

127. Then the wise woman quickly brought

128. The warrior's head so bloody

129. In the bag, which her attendant (had),

130. Fair checked for both their food, Excellent one, then she lifted the head,

131. And all gory, Prudent Judith then gave it to her handmaid to carry home.

132. Then went directly thence

133. Both courageous women

134. Until they came stout-hearted,

135. Triumphant maidens out of the pagan sanctuary.

136. That they were clearly able to see

137. The walls of the beautiful city shine,

138. Bethulia. Then they ring-adorned

139. Hastened forth on the footpath

140. Until they, joyous ones, had gotten

141. To the wall gate. Warriors sat,

142. Men on watch kept guard

143. In the fortress, as the people before

144. Sad-minded Judith commanded,

145. Wise maiden, then she departed on a journey,

146. Courageous woman. Then came again

147. Dear to the people And then the wise woman (Judith) quickly commanded

148. A certain one of the men

149. From the wide city walk towards her

150. And then quickly to let in

151. Through this wall's gate, and spoke the word to the victorious people:

152. "I may say to you, worthy of gratitude,

153. Things, that you need not mourn longer

154. In your hearts. The Lord is gracious to you,

155. Glory of Kings, that was made known

156. Through the world far and wide, Glorious success that for you

157. Splendid approaching future and Glory given

158. For the affliction which you endured for a long time."

159. Then the citizens became glad

160. After they heard how the holy one spoke

161. Over the wretched wall. The army was joyful;

162. People hastened on toward the fortress gate

163. Men and women together, in swarms and multitudes,

164. In troops and troops pressed forward and ran

165. Toward the woman in thousands,

166. Old ones and young. To the heart of each

167. Man in the mead-city (His) spirit (was) gladden.

168. Afterwards they understood that Judith was

169. Back to the homeland, and then quickly

170. With reverence they let her in.

171. Then the wise one commanded, gold adorned,

172. Her attentive handmaid

173. Unwrap the warrior's head

174. And display it as a sign, bloody to

175. The citizens, how she succeeded at Battle.

176. Then the noble one spoke to all the people:

177. "Victorious heroes, here you are able to gaze upon,

178. A leader of the people, this most hateful

179. Warrior of heathen's head.

180. Holofernes not of the living,

181. Who brought about the greatest number of killings of our people

182. Of painful sorrow, and the most still

183. Wished to add, but God did not allow him

184. Of longer life that he may torment us with afflictions;

185. I deprived him of life

186. Through God's help. Now I will ask each one of the men

187. Of the city people

188. Of the shield-bearing warriors, that you quickly

189. Send forth to battle afterwards God of Creatures

190. Merciful King, has sent from the East

191. A bright light. Carry shields forward,

192. Shields for breasts and mail coats,

193. Gleaming protection into the troop of enemies,

194. Cut down the commander with gleaming swords,

195. Fated leaders. Your enemies

196. Doomed to death, and you possess judgment,

197. Glory at battle as the

198. Mighty Lord has shown to you through my hand."

199. Then it happened the troop of bold ones quickly prepared,

200. Of the brave ones to battle. The nobly brave

201. Warriors and companions advanced, carrying triumphant banners

202. Traveled to battle forward on the straight away,

203. Heroes under the protections (helmets) from the Holy City.

204. On that same dawn; shields made a din,

205. Loudly resounded. The lean one (Beasts of battle) rejoiced in that,

206. Wolf in the forest, and the black raven,

207. Bird greedy for slaughter. Both knew

208. The men of the Nation intended to provide for them

209. A feast on the fated, moreover an eagle

210. Flew behind them eager, dewy-feathered

211. Dark-coated sang a battle song,

212. Horny-beaked. The warriors advanced,

213. Men toward battle, protected with shields,

214. Hollow (concave) shields, who while before

215. Endured the abuse of the foreigners,

216. Abuse of the heathens. That was firmly to them

217. At the spear-fight all requited,

218. After the Assyrians. The Hebrews

219. Under battle standards had advanced

220. To the camps. Then they quickly

221. Let forth fly a shower of arrows,

222. Battle-snakes from horn tipped bows,

223. Strong arrows, the fierce warriors stormed loudly

224. Sent spears,

225. Into the crowd of the cruel ones. Warriors were angry,

226. In-dwellers of the land, hostile race,

227. The stern of mood advanced, hard-hearted,

228. Aroused roughly ancient enemies

229. Besotted with mead; the warriors hands withdrew

230. From sheaths brightly adorned swords

231. Proven in edges, struck determinedly

232. The Assyrian warriors,

233. Evil schemers, not any, none,

234. The army spared, not powerful or lowly,

235. Of men alive who they were able to overcome.

236. XII So then the young retainers in the morning

237. Pursued all the foreign people for a time

238. Until they perceived who the fierce ones were,

239. The head guards of the army,

240. That the Hebrew men disclosed violent sword-play (fighting) with them.

241. They with words went to inform the

242. Old Chief thanes, aroused the warriors, and fearfully announced the dreadful news to them,

243. Besotted with mead the morning attack,

244. Terrible sword-play. Then I immediately found out (the)

245. Warriors doomed to perish shook off sleep

246. And toward the tent of the evil one, Holofernes

247. Weary-hearted crowd pressed forward,

248. They intended at once

249. To announce the battle to the lord

250. Before the terror that was with them oppressed them,

251. The Army of Hebrews. All assumed

252. That the lord of the warriors and the fair maiden

253. Were together in the beautiful tent,

254. Judith the noble one and the lecher,

255. Terrible and fierce. However, none of the noblemen

256. Who dared awake the warrior

257. Or try to discover how it had faired for the warrior

258. With the holy maiden,

259. Maiden of the Creator

260. Maiden of the Creator. (Combined with lines above)

261. Army drew near,

262. People of the Hebrews, fought severely

263. With sharp swords, repaid warfare

264. Their ancient quarrels, with decorated swords,

265. Ancient insults; Assyria's fame was diminished

266. In the day's work,

267. Pride humbled. Warriors remained

268. About the tent of their lord exceedingly troubled,

269. Downcast. Then they all together

270. Began to cough (to gain attention), to make noise loudly,

271. And gnash the teeth, without success,

272. With teeth suffered affliction. Then it was at an end their glory,

273. Prosperity and daring deeds. Then the noblemen thought to arouse

274. Their beloved lord; for they had succeeded not at all.

275. Then was tardily and belatedly a certain one to the bold of the gold-adorned

276. Need so forced him that he ventured daring(ly) into the pavilion.

277. Then he found the pale one lying dead on the bed.

278. His gold-giver deprived of spirit,

279. Deprived of life. Then he quickly fell

280. Trembling to the ground, began to tear his hair,

281. Troubled in heart, and his garment too,

282. And spoke the word to the warriors

283. The sad ones who were there outside:

284. (...combined with line above)

285. "Here is revealed to ourselves

286. Future destruction in that it is near to that time

287. With trouble near approaching which we must by necessity be lost,

288. Perish together at battle

289. Here lies dead cut down by a sword

290. Our lord beheaded." Then they sad at heart

291. Threw their weapons down, departed themselves weary-hearted

292. Hastening fled. Men fought them from behind,

293. Mighty people, until the greatest portion

294. Of the pagan sanctuary lay slain (in battle)

295. As a pleasure on the field of victory, cut down with swords,

296. For wolves and also as a comfort to slaughter greedy

297. Birds. Fled who survived,
298. Shield-warriors of hostile ones. The Hebrew army followed them on for
299. Honor with victory
300. Fame glorified; Lord god seized them
301. Beautiful in help, Lord Almighty
302. Then they quickly, with decorated swords,
303. Brave minded warriors, formed a passage
304. For the army
305. Through a throng of hostile ones, cut down the shields,
306. The wall of shields cleaved. Warriors of battle
307. Were enraged, Hebrew men;
308. Then in time the thanes severely desired
309. Battle. There in dust fell the greatest part of head-count
310. Of Assyrian nobility, Race of the hostile one; few of the alive came
311. To the native land (made it home). The nobly brave turned back,
312. Warriors on the way back, in among the carnage
313. Corpses reeking. Opportunity was to take
314. From the earth-dwellers on the hateful ones,
315. From their enemies of old not living
316. Gory booty, beautiful ornaments,
317. Shields and wide swords, shining helmets,
318. Precious treasure. They had gloriously
319. Conquered the enemies on the battlefield
320. Defenders of the homeland Ancient enemies killed by the swords
321. They rested on the trail
322. Those who of live kin were most hateful to them in life
323. Then all the nation,
324. Of the glorious woman in the space of one month,
325. Splendid one, with braided hair, carried and brought
326. To the bright city Bethulia

327. Helmets and short swords, metallic gray coats of mail,

328. Armor of men gold adorned,

329. More treasure than any

330. Of the wise ones can tell;

331. Then all the men of the nation went with courage

332. Brave ones under banners in battle

333. Through the wise teaching of Judith

334. Of the courageous maiden. They

335. Brought to reward her for the journey,

336. Noblemen brave in battle

337. The sword and sweaty helmet of Holofernes, likewise a large coat of mail

338. Ornamented with red and gold, and all that the arrogant lord of the warriors

339. Possessed of treasure or of personal inheritance,

340. Of rings and bright treasure, that they

341. Gave to the wise, bright woman.

342. For all of this Judith said

343. (Combined with line above and below)

344. Glory in the kingdom of Earth, likewise reward in heaven

345. Reward for victory in the glory of heaven, because she had true belief

346. Forever to the Almighty. Certainly at the end she did not

347. Of the reward which she yearned for a long time. For that glory be to the beloved Lord,

348. Who created wind and air, skies and spacious grounds, likewise fierce seas

349. And the delights of heaven through His own favor.

ACKNOWLEDGMENTS

A special thank you to all the teachers, mentors, friends, and family who have supported and encouraged me in my writing and throughout the study and creation of this book.

To David Ferris, Dr. Susan Kim, Tom Laird, Dr. Stella Singer, and all those at Archangel Ink who have each in their own way been an integral part of shaping this book. Without them, I would not have been able to turn Judith and her story into what they are today.

To those who have offered critical feedback and crucial encouragement, including Jan Zilkowski, Joseph Zilkowski, Rebecca Zilkowski, and Kevin Harvey.

To Bruce and Betty Zilkowski, who have encouraged my love of reading and writing from the beginning.

And most especially to Clare and Zoe, all my love.

ABOUT THE AUTHOR

S arah Zilkowski has published everything from short stories for children to travelogues. But her true passion lies in the dark ages. She has amassed 10 years of expertise in Anglo-Saxon language, literature, history and culture. *Beasts of War* is her first novel, based on her master's thesis on the *Judith* poem. She resides with her family in Cleveland, Ohio.

If you are interested in learning more about Anglo-Saxon literature, history and culture, or upcoming publications by Sarah E Zilkowski, sign-up at **JudithBook.com** for updates.